DISCD

Something stir
Something prin

Ryker moved closer, his eyes never coming off that lip she was biting. She was the most beautiful sight, and after the hellish past day and a half, he needed something beautiful in his life. He needed Laney.

His mouth slid over hers. His arms wrapped around her waist, jerking her flush against his body.

Finally.

Laney melted against him. Her mouth opened to his instantly and Ryker made no hesitation to take everything he wanted from her.

Before common sense or those red flags could wave too high, Ryker secured his hold around her waist, never breaking away from her lush mouth. He lifted her up, arousal bursting through him when she wrapped her legs around his waist.

"I didn't think you wanted me," she murmured against his lips.

Ryker spun and headed toward his room.

"I never said that. Ever."

Laney nipped at his lips. "You push me away."

Ryker stopped, pulled away and looked into those engaging eyes. "Do you feel me pushing you away now?"

* * *

Holiday Baby Surprise
is part of the Mafia Moguls series—
For this tight-knit mob family,
going legitimate leads to love!

HOLIDAY
BABY SCANDAL

BY
JULES BENNETT

First Published in Great Britain 2016
By Mills & Boon, an imprint of HarperCollins*Publishers*
1 London Bridge Street, London, SE1 9GF

© 2016 Jules Bennett

ISBN: 978-0-263-06578-7

Our policy is to use papers that are natural, renewable and recyclable
products and made from wood grown in sustainable forests. The logging
and manufacturing processes conform to the legal environmental
regulations of the country of origin.

Printed and bound in Great Britain
by CPI Antony Rowe, Chippenham, Wiltshire

To all the readers who've asked about Ryker…
you're welcome.

One

With one hand clutching the forgotten cuff links and one hand firmly over her still-flat stomach, Laney pulled in a deep breath and willed courage to make an appearance.

She was an O'Shea, damn it. She didn't back down in the face of fear. Fear was nothing but a lie. A bold-faced lie capable of defeating most people. Laney wasn't most people.

She'd come this far, all she had to do was knock…and make a life-changing confession to a man she'd been in love with since she was old enough to notice boys. Forget the fact he'd been ten years older. Age meant about as much to her as fear did.

Tears clogged her throat as emotions threatened to overwhelm her. Whatever his reaction, she owed him the truth. But if he rejected her, the pain would slice deep.

Laney pushed aside the hurt, the fear and the nausea, and pounded on Ryker Barrett's front door.

No turning back now.

Ryker had been part of her life since she was a child. He'd worked for her father, was best friends with her brothers. Her family had taken him in when his own had turned him away. He was mysterious, intriguing and frustrating.

And for the past five weeks he'd been pretending nothing had happened. He gave no hint that he even recalled tearing her Chanel dress from her body before holding her against her hotel room wall and bringing her every desire to life.

Nope. It was business as usual. When she'd had to feed him information via email or text for O'Shea's auctions, he'd never given any indication that their one heated night had made an impact on his life whatsoever. Was he that emotionally detached?

Well, he was about to sustain one hell of an impact. He may try to ignore her, but there was no way he could ignore the consequences of their night.

The door swung open and the entire speech she'd rehearsed all morning vanished from her mind. Ryker stood before her wearing only a pair of running shorts, a tatted chest and glorious muscle tone.

She'd never seen him this way. The man who traveled the globe in designer suits, the man who donned a leather jacket and worn jeans to blend in when necessary, had never presented himself in such a beautiful, natural manner. He should do this more often.

Casual as you please, Ryker rested a forearm on the edge of the door and quirked a brow as if she'd disturbed him. Yeah, well, he deserved to be put out. She'd been fighting her feelings for him for years.

Rage bubbled from within as she slapped his cuff links against his bare chest and pushed past him. In all the years she'd known him, Laney had never come to his house in Boston. When they met, it was always on neutral ground, usually at the O'Shea family home her brother Braden now lived in.

As infuriating as Ryker could be, Laney was the first to admit that her family would crumble without him. He may be the "enforcer," the guy who kept them protected and took the brunt of any backlash they ever faced, but he could easily cut ties and leave. This billionaire never threw his money around like most men she knew. Loyalty meant much more to Ryker than finances ever would… one of the many reasons she was drawn to him.

The door closed at her back. Laney shut her eyes and tried to forget the intensity of their complicated relationship, tried to ignore the way her body instantly responded to this man. She was here for one reason. And the fact that he worked for her family, was practically *part* of her family, wasn't making this confession any easier.

"If you're here regarding the painting in L.A. that you emailed me about last week, I've already—"

Laney whirled. "I'm not here about work."

Crossing his arms over his broad chest, Ryker widened his stance and gave a brief nod. "I can't believe it took you this long to come to me."

Laney's heart kicked up. So he knew she would bring up that night, and he'd what? Been waiting on her? Jerk. Uncaring, unfeeling, stupid, sexy jerk. Why couldn't he put a shirt on? She was trying to keep her anger going, but lust was creeping into the mix.

"You could've come to me," she threw back. "Or, I don't know, actually talked to me when we were exchanging work information."

The O'Sheas were a force all their own, known around the globe for their prestigious auction houses. Laney had ignored the whispered "mafia" or "mob" rumors her entire life. She knew full well what her family was, and she was a proud member. They remained on the right side of the law thanks to the connections her late father had made and the ones her brother Braden, who was now in charge, and her other brother Mac continued to work at.

And Ryker Barrett, other than starring in her every fantasy for years, was the family's right-hand man, security detail and any other job they needed him for. He did the dirty work and lay low, staying out of the limelight and behind the scenes.

Laney waited for him to say something, anything, but he stood there staring at her, which only made her nerves worse. How could he have so much power over her? She was an O'Shea, for crying out loud, and he was just standing there.

Standing there looking all half-naked, sexy and perfect.

Focus, Laney.

Ryker held up the cuff links. "Was this all?"

Laney narrowed her eyes. "Am I interrupting something?"

Or someone? It hadn't even occurred to her that he may be entertaining. A sick feeling in the pit of her stomach grew, and she hated the spear of jealousy that ripped through her.

"Yeah, my morning session with the punching bag."

Which explained those perfectly sculpted arms, shoulders and pecs, though Laney figured he used a punching bag as a means of releasing his emotions rather than to stay in shape. Ryker was the epitome of keeping to himself and never letting anyone get too close. So what did that say about that night they shared? Clearly he'd thrown all of his rules out the window because they'd been as close as two people could get.

Nausea pushed its way to the front of the line, bypassing her worry, her fear. Laney closed her eyes, waiting to see if she needed to find the bathroom or take a seat and let the wave pass. *Please, please, just pass.* Of all times to appear vulnerable, this was not the one.

"Listen, I get you want to discuss what happened," he began, oblivious to her current state. "I take the blame. I shouldn't have followed you into your room and—"

"Ripped my clothes off?" she finished, holding a hand to her stomach and glaring across the room at him. "I'm not sorry it happened. I've been waiting on you to notice I'm not just Mac and Braden's little sister. I've fantasized about you ripping my clothes off, and I don't even mind that you ruined my favorite dress. So, I'm not sorry a bit. I'm only sorry about how you treated me after."

Other than the muscles ticking in his stubbled jaw, Ryker showed no emotion.

"This wasn't just some one-night stand," she argued.

"It was."

Okay. That hurt—the truth often did—but still. They were more, so much more, than a quick, albeit amazing, romp.

"How dare you act like I was just some random stranger?" she yelled, throwing her arms out wide. "I've known you almost my whole life. You think it's okay to have sex with me and—"

He moved in a flash, gripped her shoulders and hauled her against his bare chest. "No, I didn't think it was okay, but I couldn't stop. Damn it, Laney."

Ryker released her and took a step back, letting her go as if she'd burned him. "I couldn't stop," he whispered.

She had to get out of here. The last time they'd been alone his control had snapped, and he was barely hanging on by a thread now that she was in his living room, on his turf.

He'd purposely been avoiding her since their one-night stand, only communicating through texts for stuff related to O'Shea's. They'd been working together for the past several years. He could admit that when she came on board, his job had become so much easier. With her being able to dig deeper, to infiltrate systems he never could've…she was invaluable. Laney's computer hacking skills were eerily good. If she ever worked with the wrong crowd, she could be dangerous. Granted, some considered the O'Sheas the wrong crowd, but whatever. He couldn't do his job without her, so avoiding her altogether wasn't an option.

The torture of working so close together was worth it, though. Even the slightest communication with Laney kept him going. He shouldn't enjoy the pain of being so near, unable to fulfill his every desire, but he chalked up his masochistic tendencies to his less than stellar childhood.

When he wasn't on assignment, he typically would hide out at his home in London or take a trip to some random destination just because he could and had no ties. When he was in Boston, he was too tempted to give in to his desires for his best friends' and bosses' little sister.

When Laney started to reach for him, Ryker held up a hand. "No." If she touched him, this whole distance thing would crumble. He'd been playing with fire when he'd grabbed her a second ago...but damn if she didn't feel good against him.

This had to stop. He owed it to the family who saved him from a living hell. For years he'd ached for her, watched from afar as she grew into a breathtaking woman who managed to slip beneath his defenses. When she'd dated other men, it had nearly gutted him, but what right did he have to say anything?

She was the mafia princess, and he was the family... problem solver. He'd been involved with a lot of dark deeds before her father passed away and left the family business to Braden. Now they were all on the path to being legitimate. But legitimacy didn't change what he'd done in the past. And no matter that his bank account had more zeroes than any one person would need, that didn't change the fact he wasn't worthy of Laney. Not only was she the daughter of one of Boston's most powerful men, but she'd never made it a secret she wanted a large family, complete with babies and pets. He opted for lovers in other states and countries, to keep things physical and void of all emotions.

To put things simply, they were on opposite ends of this warped world. Since Patrick's death months ago, Braden and Mac protected her, and rightfully so, from the harsh realities their family faced each day. Actually, Laney's protection had also been part of Ryker's job.

Not that he needed the money or the job. But he owed the O'Sheas. Anything they asked for, he would provide or die trying. And it was all of that watching over Laney that had damn near done him in.

Blowing out a breath, he shook his head and faced her, but froze. Laney had stepped back and was leaning against the wall. Her closed eyes, her long, slow breaths had him narrowing the distance between them.

"Laney?" He was near enough to touch her, but kept his hands to himself. See? He could do it. He'd just be right here in case she needed something…like his hands on her.

With shaky fingers, he shoved her hair away from her face. Her lids fluttered open, but a sheen of sweat had popped up over her forehead. Was she that nervous about being here?

"I know you don't want me here, but I have to tell you something."

She pushed from the wall, swaying slightly.

Now he didn't resist contact. Ryker grabbed her around the waist and held her against him. "Are you all right?"

"Let me go."

Those vibrant green eyes came up to meet his. The punch to his gut instantly forced him back to that night, to her pinned between his body and the wall. She'd panted his name as she'd clung to his back. Never had he experienced anything so…perfect. And he didn't deserve one second of her affection. Mac and Braden would kick his ass if they knew… Well, they'd try, anyway. He could handle himself in a fight, but he deserved at least a punch to the face over the way he'd seduced Laney like she was just another woman he'd met on one of his trips. Laney was nothing like those other women, and he needed to remember that.

Ryker dropped his hands but didn't step back. He couldn't, not when she still seemed so unsteady and his body was wound so tightly. She was a drug, his drug. They were bad for each other for too many reasons, yet he wanted more.

"I'm pregnant."

Ryker stilled. Had she just…

What the hell? He hadn't heard her right. No way. When they'd been in Miami, he hadn't planned on having sex with her after the party at the new O'Shea's location, but she'd assured him she was on birth control. So, no. He hadn't heard right.

But Laney continued to stare up at him, and Ryker waited for her to say something else, anything else, because there was no way in hell…

"I'm sorry." Laney leaned her head back against the wall and shut her eyes once more. "I didn't know how else to say it. I mean, there's really no good lead-in to something like this."

Pregnant. As in, a baby. Their baby.

Ryker turned away as dread consumed him. How the hell had he allowed something like this to even be a possibility? A child was definitely not something he ever wanted in his life. No damn way would he purposely bring an innocent baby into this world. Into his darkness.

"You said you were on birth control."

He didn't mean for the words to come out as an accusation, but he was confused, damn it. And angry. Angry at himself, because had he kept that control of his in line, Laney wouldn't be dropping this bomb.

"I was." She pulled in a breath and squared her shoulders. "I had to switch the one I was on and started a new one the week before Miami. I don't know if that's why it happened. I just don't know…"

He remembered so clearly her tugging his shirt over

his head and telling him she was on birth control, that she had just had a physical and was clean. He knew full well he hadn't been with anyone for a while, and he'd never gone without protection. So in their frantic state of shedding clothes and getting to the good stuff, they'd had a two-second conversation about contraception.

So here they were. Laney was expecting his child and he was…screwed. Literally.

Bracing his hands on the antique table behind the sofa, Ryker dropped his head. He'd kept his hands, and all his other parts, to himself this whole time. Out of respect for the family who took him in and saved his life, Ryker hadn't given in to the one desire he'd had for years. Until Miami, damn it. How would he ever make things right with the O'Sheas?

Patrick had taken Ryker in at the age of twelve when Ryker had stood up for Braden and Mac on the playground, and the boys had become best friends. Ryker had instantly become like family, but he'd never thought of Laney as a sister. At the time, he'd ignored her because she was so much younger. But by the time she graduated high school, Ryker was deep in the family business, and more than aware that his dirty hands should never touch the sophisticated Laney O'Shea.

When her computer hacking skills were made apparent, Ryker knew she'd be an asset. He'd just had no idea how difficult it would be to work with her. He could afford to hire anyone to do the behind-the-screen work, but he trusted only her.

Braden and Mac were going to kill him. They would kill him and bury his body, and no one would ever know…and he deserved nothing less.

Damn it. Ryker blew out a breath. This was how he

repaid the family who trusted him, who was loyal to him when no one else cared?

"This isn't your fault."

Her soft voice washed over him, and he let out a curt laugh. "No? Am I the one who pushed his way into your room, tore that dress off and demanded you wrap your legs around me? Or was that another man?"

He threw her a glance just in time to see her flinch. Great. Now he was being an ass. All of this was on him. Laney didn't deserve his anger—she was just as innocent as the child.

His gaze dropped to her flat stomach, and fear engulfed him. Images of his biological father flooded his mind, and Ryker vowed that second to never be that man. Never would he lay a hand on his child, never would he choose the next fix over putting food on the table.

Ryker's childhood may be a sad cliché, but that was life and all too often kids were mistreated while other adults turned a blind eye to the abuse.

Ryker looked down. Random scars covered his knuckles, his forearms. His life was made up of more ugly than anything else, yet this beautiful, vibrant woman stood here giving him something so precious and all he wanted to do was...

Hell. What did he want to do? He never wanted Braden or Mac to find out about the night he'd spent with their baby sister. Not that he was afraid of them. He could handle anything thrown his way—almost anything.

They trusted Ryker to keep the family safe, to keep all threats away. Wasn't that why he'd been ordered to follow her back to her hotel that night? Because there had been a threat against her?

For years he'd kept asshats away from her. A few

months ago he'd had to use physical force and pull some major strings to get her ex out of her life. The man had made a menace of himself and had started harassing Laney. He hadn't told Laney what happened, and he never would, but he knew she wondered. Wondered if Ryker had done something sinister. And maybe that was for the best. Maybe she wouldn't get those stars in her eyes like she'd had when they were intimate in Miami.

Pushing off the table, Ryker ran a hand down his face. Stubble rustled beneath his palm, and he honestly had no idea what to do next. He'd never faced something this life-altering, this damn scary.

"I don't expect anything from you." Laney stood straight, apparently feeling better. Her coloring was back. "But I wasn't going to keep this a secret, either. I know you don't want anything to do with me—"

"Stop saying that," he growled. "You have no idea what I want."

She tipped up her head, quirked a brow, as if issuing a silent challenge. "Enlighten me."

If only things were that easy. If only their relationship was about sex and nothing else. *If only* was the story of his entire messed-up life.

"I will be here for this child," he told her, turning to face her fully. "I'll keep you protected."

"You've been looking out for me for years."

He took a step forward. "Not like this. If you think I was protective before, you haven't seen anything."

Laney rolled her eyes. "Don't do this. Don't be over-bearing. If I hadn't gotten pregnant, I know you would've gone on to ignore me on a personal level. That night we spent together wasn't supposed to happen, but we were on that path for so long, it was inevitable."

He hated when she was right. Hated even more that every night since then, he'd had to replay it over and over in his mind because he would never be that close to her again. And she'd ruined him for any other woman.

"I can take care of the baby and myself just fine." She glared back. "But I don't want my brothers to know just yet. I'm not ready."

As much as he hated hiding from anything that threatened him, he was in total agreement. Braden and Mac would find out soon enough, but for now, just no. First, he and Laney had to grasp this news themselves.

Ryker took another step until the gap between them was closed. "Let's get something straight now. I will take care of you and our baby. You need anything, I'm providing it. You won't shut me out. If I have to haul you off to my home in London and watch you personally, I will."

Laney snorted. "Really? Now you choose to let me in?"

"I don't have a choice," he muttered.

And maybe he never had…not where Laney was concerned.

So how the hell did he even attempt to keep his loyalty to this family when he'd betrayed them? And how was he going to be closer to Laney than ever before and keep his hands off her?

Ryker Barrett had lived through some rough times, but he had a feeling he was entering a whole new level of hell.

Two

How cute was he, thinking he could be all protective and overbearing? Poor Ryker. He clearly forgot he was dealing with an O'Shea. She may be the baby sister, she may be the one everyone loved to keep safely tucked away behind the computer, but she knew more than they'd ever realize. She wasn't naive, and she wasn't blind.

And going to London? Not an option. She was working on something right here in Boston that was so near to her heart, she refused to walk away. Pregnant or not, she'd see this project come to fruition.

Once she'd left Ryker's house earlier, she headed home, changed her clothes and went for a run. Her doctor had informed her that keeping up with her regular exercise routine was perfectly fine. She needed to release some pent-up energy and blow off steam anyway. Perhaps she should've joined Ryker in his punching bag workout. Although she feared he'd have pissed her off and she'd have ended up socking him in the face to knock some sense into that thick head of his.

Why did she have to be attracted to such a stubborn, frustrating man? Why did she still have to feel how amazing he was weeks after their encounter? The imprint of his powerful touch would be with her forever. Laney had always wondered if the reality of being with Ryker would measure up to the fantasy...and it was better. So much better than anything she could have dreamed up.

But now that she was pregnant, she wasn't going to use the child as an excuse to get closer to him. She wasn't a pathetic, desperate woman. She may have loved Ryker for as long as she could remember, but she would never use an innocent child to get a man.

She'd worried about telling him, though. Worried because she knew enough of his childhood to figure out he probably had no dreams of becoming a father. Ryker never spoke of his birth family—his family had become the O'Sheas the instant Mac and Braden brought him home after school one day. All she knew was that his first twelve years had been hell, and nothing any child should have to go through.

Ryker may be ten years older than her, but that didn't make him out of her reach. By the time she'd been old enough to notice boys, she'd had eyes for only one man. Oh, she'd dated, but nobody had captured her attention like Ryker. And for years he'd ignored her.

Then one night, as if the dam had broken, he'd quite literally torn off her clothes. Never had Laney been so thrilled, so relieved to finally have a dream become reality. But no dream could've ever prepared her for the experience Ryker gave her.

Laney pulled her damp hair into a loose topknot. Now that she'd exercised and showered, she was ready to get some work done. Her brothers were so close to finding their family's missing heirlooms, and she so wanted to be the one to crack the mystery.

For years, decades actually, their family had been searching for nine missing scrolls. The precious documents dated back to the sixteenth century, when one of their ancestors, an Irish monk, transcribed some of William Shakespeare's work. The scrolls had been handed down from generation to generation.

But when the Great Depression robbed so many people of their normal lives, the O'Shea family lost their home and everything inside. The home actually ended up falling into the possession of Zara Perkins's family, which was how Zara and Braden met. Braden had thought that cozying up to the pretty event coordinator and getting inside her house would help in their search. Little did Braden know he'd fall in love.

The scrolls weren't found, so now the search continued. And Laney would love nothing more than to be the one to find the missing treasure. Her entire life she'd been sheltered, kept at an arm's length from the dangers of the family business. If her father and brothers hadn't needed her mad computer skills, she had no doubt they wouldn't have told her a single thing.

Well, if she found these scrolls, they'd have to acknowledge just how much she brought to the table and how she wasn't afraid to get her hands dirty. Family meant everything, and, now more than ever, she was determined to take a stronger role in the business. Proving to her brothers, to Ryker, that she could keep up with them wasn't going to be a problem. She was an

O'Shea. Determination was ingrained in every fiber of her being.

Laney pulled up her email and slid a hand over her flat stomach. This baby would be so hardheaded and strong. There was no other option, considering the genes.

Scrolling through messages, Laney tried to forget Ryker and his demanding ways. But it was those demanding ways that had rocked her entire world at a hotel in Miami.

Maybe she could distract herself with some online Christmas shopping. Maybe that would take her mind off Ryker and the fact she now carried his child. Laney couldn't help but wonder how her overbearing brothers would react to this news.

Dread filled her stomach. How would Zara take the pregnancy? She and Braden had miscarried a child several months ago. Were they trying for another one? Laney hated to pry, but she also didn't want to seem insensitive. Especially if they tried and were unsuccessful.

Oh, they'd be happy about the baby, but privately would they be hurt? Laney loved Zara like a sister and didn't want to cause her any more grief.

With Mac and Jenna planning a wedding, Laney seriously hesitated to say anything to anybody. There wouldn't be a perfect time, but at least she could wait for a better time.

Laney clicked on an email she'd been waiting on. Her offer had been accepted. Finally. She'd been wanting this news for over a week, and the timing was perfect. One more step closer to her goal of revamping an old, run-down building in Boston's south side... Ryker's old neighborhood.

She'd set these plans in motion before Miami. Over

the years, she'd heard Ryker talk about unfortunate kids, never of his own childhood, but she knew his worry stemmed from where he'd come from. So Laney wanted to help. She hated the idea of kids feeling like there was no hope, no one there who really cared about their future.

Her father had instilled in her that commitment. To help the unfortunate. When he'd taken in Ryker, he'd done so without another thought. If more people reached out like her father had, maybe this world would be a bit brighter.

She was keeping the project a secret because she wasn't in it for the praise or the recognition. And she definitely wasn't out to make the O'Shea name look better in the community, which was what many would think if they knew she was involved.

Laney starred the email and laid her phone on the desk in her office before taking a seat. It had gotten so dark since she'd finished her run. She longed for summer and sunshine, where she didn't have to worry about getting back in time before sunset. She also wondered if running alone was the smartest choice. She always had done it by herself to clear her head and think, but now that she was pregnant, she felt more vulnerable.

From the time she was little, her father had taught her to always be aware of her surroundings. But now she should take a few more precautions. Even though she lived in Boston and the streets were bustling with people, she might want to consider using her treadmill or finding a jogging partner.

A laugh escaped her as she thought of Ryker. She couldn't quite imagine the brooding man throwing on a pair of sneakers and running. No, he was more of a boxer type, a guy who lifted heavy weights, or did pull-ups with one arm. He was all strength, all power.

And the thought of all of that excellent muscle tone had Laney attempting to focus on something else. Anything.

Christmas shopping. Right. That's what she'd been planning to do. Why go to the stores and fight all the crazies when she could go braless at home and have everything delivered right to her door...wrapped even.

Online shopping was glorious.

She also had a few final touches to put on the O'Shea's holiday party they were having for the staff at Braden's house in two weeks. The annual event had grown even more since Mac had opened satellite offices in Miami and Atlanta.

Still, Laney loved working on the party and Zara was a professional coordinator, so her sister-in-law had done the majority of the work this year. Laney just needed to order the centerpieces she and Zara had agreed on.

She'd just opened a new browser to search for a dress to wear to the party when her doorbell rang. Glancing quickly at the monitors, she saw Ryker's hulking frame. He kept his head down, shoulders hunched against the brisk December air. He never came to her house...just like she had never gone to his. He'd followed her home before to make sure she was safe, but he'd never popped in of his own accord.

Who knew it would take a pregnancy to get him to come for a visit?

Pushing away from her desk, Laney headed toward the front door. Darkness had set in and snow swirled around, bright flakes catching in the streetlights.

Laney flicked the lock on her door and opened it, immediately stepping back so Ryker could come in out of the cold.

Without a word he strode inside. Those heavy black boots were quite the contrast to her bare feet with polished pink toes. And that was barely the beginning of all the ways they differed.

Laney closed out the cold and set the dead bolt. Crossing her arms over her chest, she faced the man she'd been half in love with since she was a teen.

"This is a surprise," she told him. "Did you come to talk or is something wrong?"

"I need to head out of town."

Laney nodded. His rushing out of town was nothing new. He did so many things for the family. The O'Sheas had gone global with their famous auction houses. Ryker sometimes traveled to obtain relics or random pieces for a specific auction. He'd been known to procure heirlooms that had been stolen. Some may look at him as a modern-day Robin Hood since he returned items to their right owner.

He also was known to go to his home in London for a quick escape, but he was always a text or call away. He put her family first above all else.

"I'm leaving in the morning, and I'll be gone a few days."

Laney tipped up her head. "You never tell me when you're going out of town unless you need my computer skills to pull up the blueprint of a building. If that's what you—"

"I'm not here for the blueprint."

The way those black-as-night eyes held her in place had her shivering. Why did she let him have such power over her? He had more power in one stare than most guys did in a kiss. And she'd dated some great kissers.

"Then why are you here?" She was proud of her strong tone but worried about what his answer would be.

"Are you feeling okay?" he asked, his eyes dropping to her stomach, then back up. "I didn't ask earlier. Or, hell, maybe I did. It's all still kind of a blur."

So he was here about the pregnancy. She should've known he wouldn't stay too far from her. He'd always been protective in that overbearing, bouncer kind of way.

"If you're going to hover, don't waste your time."

She didn't want to sound ungrateful, but she didn't want a babysitter. She wanted him, damn it. She wanted him to see her as a woman. As the woman he'd let down his guard with several weeks ago.

Up until then, she'd always thought he saw her as Mac and Braden's little sister. Someone he helped when necessary, but who was more family than anything.

"If I want to hover, I damn well will," he growled. "You're having my child. You're part of a very well-known family, and it's my job to protect you."

That was the crux of the entire problem. The slice to her heart shouldn't surprise her. Did she honestly think that after they'd had sex he'd come around? That when he knew about the baby he'd profess his undying love to her? No, but she'd at least hoped for him to treat her like…hell. Was it too much to ask for him to act like he cared about her as more than his friends' baby sister?

"I don't want to be your job."

Laney turned before he could see the hurt on her face. Heading back toward her office, she couldn't care less if he let himself out or if he followed. Trying to capture

Ryker's attention for so long was exhausting. She sure as hell didn't want it now due to a job or a baby. She wanted him to look at her for her. Nothing else.

Apparently that was too much to ask. With his traveling schedule, he probably did hookups and one-night stands. She'd never seen him in any type of a relationship or even heard him mention seeing someone. Laney thought she may take way too much delight in that, but whatever.

Just as she reached the threshold of her office, a hand clamped around her arm and spun her.

"Don't walk away from me."

Laney raised her brows. "You're not in charge of me, no matter what my brothers tell you to do. I can get along just fine without being coddled."

"Would you quit acting like you're so put out? Your brothers care about you and only want you safe."

Laney jerked free of his hold but kept her eyes on his. "And what about you, Ryker? Do you care about me?"

"Of course I do."

Laney swallowed. "As a brother?"

The muscles along the stubbled jaw ticked. "I'm not doing this, Laney. I'm not hashing out my feelings or letting you get inside my head."

Of course he wouldn't. Ryker would never let anyone in because he was made of steel. She'd never seen him show emotion, other than frustration and anger. But he never talked about what drove him to those feelings. The clenching of the muscles in his perfectly squared jaw indicated he was angry. Other than that, he played his cards seriously close to his chest.

"Whatever." She waved a hand in the air. "I'm feeling fine. There. Now you've checked up on me, and you can go on your way, guilt-free. This all could've been done in a text."

"Maybe," he agreed. "But if you were feeling bad you'd lie, and I wanted to see for myself."

Laney went for broke. "I think we both know between the two of us who would lie about how they feel."

When he remained still, silent, Laney was done. They were getting nowhere, and she wasn't in the mood to play games or whatever the hell else he wanted.

"I won't keep you out of the baby's life, but I don't want your attention just because I'm pregnant. I've waited for years for you to notice me. I thought Miami was something, but I was clearly mistaken, since you ignored me until you knew I was having your child."

All of that was so hard to admit, but at this point what did she have to lose? She wasn't one to hide her feelings, which only made Ryker squirm. Good. He deserved it.

The second she jerked the door open, a burst of cold air rushed in. "If you're done here…"

Laney turned and stared out at the blowing flakes. She didn't want to look at him, not when she still craved him. Putting up some type of emotional barrier was the only way she'd survive this.

Heavy boots moved across her hardwood floor. Ryker stopped right in front of her but kept his gaze out the open door. Laney stared at his black, leather-clad shoulder. The smell of his jacket, the familiar woodsy cologne and the unmistakable scent that she only associated with Ryker assaulted her senses. Why did he have to be the one to hold her emotionally captive?

"I've noticed you," he whispered as he remained rooted inches from her. "I've noticed too much for too long."

Laney's breath caught in her throat.

"But Miami won't happen again." Turning, he locked those dark eyes on her. "I'll check on you while I'm away."

And then he was gone. Shoulders hunched against the blowing snow, head down, Ryker walked off her porch and down the walk toward his car. Despite shivering, Laney waited until he was in the SUV with the engine running before she closed the door...but not before she caught him looking back at her.

Just that glance from a distance was enough to have her stomach doing flops, her heart pounding.

Ryker may be checking on her because of the baby, something she couldn't be upset about, but his telling words gave her hope. He'd noticed her. And from the way he seemed to be angry about it, he'd clearly been fighting with himself over the fact for a while now.

Laney leaned back against her door and wrapped her arms around her abdomen. She had no idea what was going to happen now that she and Ryker were on this journey, but one thing was perfectly clear. They were in this together, whether he liked it or not.

Three

"I don't like this."

Ryker's cell phone lay on the console as he watched the house across the street. With Braden on speaker, Ryker could focus on who was coming and going.

"I'm not a fan myself, but I think there's something here," Ryker replied.

This was his first interaction with Braden since Ryker discovered Laney was expecting. The guilt of his betrayal weighed heavily on his chest. The O'Sheas had been everything to him over the years, and he'd purposely kept his distance from Laney because he knew what would happen if he touched her. Just one touch, that's all it would've taken at any given time for him to snap.

But she'd mouthed off at the party and between her sass and that body-hugging dress, his self-control had finally expired.

Damn, the woman could tempt a saint…not that he

was anywhere near that holy. But he'd completely lost it in Miami. Years of pent-up frustration, the fact she'd been receiving threats and not sharing that information, and the way she'd looked in that short black dress had been the combination for his undoing.

"How long are you going to wait?" Braden's low tone cut through the memories.

Ryker rubbed the penny between his thumb and index finger, hating the way he carried the damn thing around like some good-luck charm. He was pathetic for even still having it, but the reminder of where he came from always needed to be front and center.

"I've seen a member of the DeLuca family go in, but nothing else."

The DeLuca family was known for organized crime. Thugs, actually. They didn't even compare to the O'Sheas, though Ryker thought some members of law enforcement would lump the two families in the same category…or prison cell.

"What activity has Laney uncovered?" Braden asked.

Ryker raked a hand down his face. "She's seen some email chatter with several family members discussing moving a package. When she dug a little deeper, she found they have an old trunk in the basement that contains some documents. But we have no clue what they are."

Ryker didn't know how the coveted scrolls would've ended up hours away from where they were last seen or how they were in a basement belonging to an organized crime family, but this was the strongest lead they'd had in a while. Ryker had followed every tip that had popped up. He'd been to London twice, Mexico, Paris and several US states.

When Patrick passed several months ago, he had one dying request. He wanted the scrolls found and returned to the O'Shea family. He'd tried for years to recover them but to no avail. Ryker fully intended to finish the job... it was the least he could do for the people to whom he owed his life.

"Damn, Laney is calling me," Braden stated. "Keep me posted no matter what happens or what time it is."

Laney was calling? Was she okay? Did something happen?

Every time he'd thought of her since Miami, all he could think about was the way she came apart in his arms. She'd been so responsive, so passionate. Now when he thought of her, all he could think was that she was carrying his child. His. Child.

The words didn't seem real even in his own mind. How the hell was he going to take care of a baby? What did he know? His father had only taught him how to get high, get laid and steal. The essentials of every childhood according to dear ole Dad.

Ryker kept his eyes on the house, but his mind wasn't on the job. Damn. This was why he never got involved with anyone. His loyalties were with Braden and Mac now. And by default, as their baby sister, Laney. If he was worrying about anyone, especially a woman, he wouldn't be able to concentrate on the task at hand. And the task sure as hell wasn't Laney.

She'd called Braden, not Ryker. That shouldn't bother him, but it did. There was no denying that he wanted to be the one she called on when she needed anything. But he couldn't be that deep in her life and keep his distance at the same time.

His mind went into overdrive. If something was going

on with the baby, she wouldn't have called Braden, that much Ryker was sure of.

Ryker disconnected the call. The penny was heavy in his hand. Over the years, he'd tried to tell himself that the souvenir from the best day of his life was ridiculous and childish to keep. Yet each day he left his house, he grabbed his keys and the penny and shoved them in his pocket. He couldn't seem to let go of his past.

Story of his life.

After another hour of waiting, which brought the grand total up to six, Ryker decided to call it a night. Laney would let him know if more activity came through her. She'd managed to tap into several areas: emails, private messages on social media, a cell phone.

Ryker always marveled at how crazy brilliant she was. She was seriously the brains behind the operation when it came to research and hunting down people. For years, she'd managed to find anything online, while Ryker did the grunt work. They were a team in a sense, but he never wanted to look at things that way. If he did, then he'd have to admit there was a relationship. And even when their dealings had been platonic, he couldn't analyze things too deeply when it came to Laney.

The woman could make a man forget everything else in this ugly world. She had beauty, grace and a stubborn streak he couldn't help but admire.

And now she was having his baby.

Pulling himself up straighter in his seat, Ryker brought the engine of his SUV to life. Snow covered the streets and showed no sign of stopping soon. December in New York was just as brutal and unpredictable as in Boston.

Cranking up the heat, he maneuvered through the

streets toward the hotel. Another cold hotel. He always booked a suite. Mostly because growing up he'd lived in a one-room dump of an apartment. Now that he could afford to stay anywhere or buy anything he wanted, he fully intended to take advantage.

But he'd never look at another hotel the same after Miami. Laney changed everything.

He couldn't even wrap his mind around the fact he was going to be a father. What the hell did he know? His own father had used him as a punching bag when he was awake and only half drunk. Ryker never wanted marriage, kids, the minivan experience. He was just fine with the job he had. Though Braden and Mac would never tell him this was a job, to them he was simply a brother, a best friend.

Which made this pregnancy so much harder to comprehend. He couldn't come to grips with how he should deal with it, so how the hell could he figure out how to tell them?

Laney was such an innocent. They'd worked for years to keep her safe, to keep her behind the scenes. Ryker had made enemies all over the globe. Now that Laney was pregnant, he would have to be twice as diligent about keeping those he cared about safe.

Yeah, he cared about her. Too much. Being ten years older than her, he'd not paid much attention when he first came to the O'Sheas as a teen. Then he'd been out of the house mostly doing grunt work and earning his way in the family, so he didn't have to go back to his former hellhole.

By the time he'd started coming around the house more often, Laney was a teen herself and he was a bastard for looking at her twice. If Patrick O'Shea had ever thought Ryker was eyeing his daughter, Ryker doubted he'd still be here.

But Ryker had respected the man more than anyone. Patrick had shown him what a true father figure was. Patrick had cared for his children, put them first and kept them protected at all costs. He had demanded loyalty, and there was nothing Ryker had wanted to give him more.

Which was one of the main reasons he wanted to be the one to uncover the scrolls. Patrick was gone, but Ryker still wanted to do this one final job for the only real father he'd ever known.

And all the more reason Ryker needed to keep his hands to himself where Laney was concerned. Patrick had been extremely protective and cautious when Laney wanted to date certain men. There were guys who wanted to date her simply for her last name or because they thought they could get into the family and wanted to use her as a warped version of a job interview.

Ryker had done neither of those things. He'd just gone straight to taking her against a wall and getting her pregnant like a loser.

One thing was for sure. He may not be father material, but he wasn't about to ignore his responsibilities. If he had his way, he'd whisk Laney and their baby away and tuck them safely in his home in London...or he'd buy a damn private island. Anything to keep them safe.

He had the funds, that wasn't the problem. No, the problem came in the form of a beautiful, stubborn, Irish goddess who would rather argue with him than listen to reason.

Ryker pulled into a parking spot right outside the window to his room. Always on the ground floor, always near an exit.

Fear overwhelmed him for the first time in years. Not for himself but for Laney and their unborn child.

When he got back to Boston, they were going to have to talk. He couldn't outrun her any longer. He may not want a relationship with her, or anyone else for that matter, but he'd make damn sure she was taken care of... regardless of the cost to his own heart.

Most would say he didn't have a heart. Ryker would have to agree. But Laney made him feel, and he could see the train wreck coming. Someone was going to get hurt.

When Laney had called her brother because her Christmas decorations were too heavy for her to lift, she hadn't even realized the time of night. But here he was hauling box after box into her living room.

"Why do you have so much stuff to put up for only one month?" he growled as he sat the last box beside her sofa.

"So you can enjoy it when you come to visit." Laney smiled and patted his cheek. "Just think, in about four weeks you can come back and take this all back up to my attic."

"I'll hire someone. Hell, just leave it up all year long. I won't judge."

Laney pulled the lid off one box and stared down at the contents. Christmas decorations were her crack. She loved everything about them. The lights, the glass ornaments that belonged to her mother, the garland she strung over her mantel and down her staircase. Everything was so magical, so perfect, and it made her remember how amazing her childhood had been. A house full of family and laughter, the parties they'd thrown in the O'Shea ballroom.

Tears pricked her eyes. She wanted that for her baby.

She wanted her child to know the meaning of family gatherings. There was nothing more valuable to Laney than her family. She needed them now more than ever, but she had no idea how to tell them a little O'Shea was about to join their ranks.

She wasn't afraid of how they'd react to the baby; her brothers would welcome another O'Shea. But how would they treat Ryker? He was such a staple in their family, and he was so much more to Braden and Mac than just an employee. He was…everything.

Laney sighed and blinked back tears.

"Hey, you okay?" Braden stood beside her, bending to look her in the eye. "Oh, damn. Please don't cry. I'll help take them down later, I swear."

Why was it that the strongest of men couldn't handle a little water?

"I'm fine," she assured him, waving a hand. "It's late and I'm tired. That's all."

His dark brows raised in disbelief. "And you opted to start decorating now?"

"I've got a lot on my mind." Wasn't that an understatement. "I'll work on this until I think I can fall asleep."

Crossing his arms over his chest, Braden straightened and pinned her with his eyes. "Is there a problem I need to know about?"

Laney picked up an ornament and began to peel away its bubble wrap. "Just worrying about my brothers. Nothing new."

That wasn't a total lie. She always worried about them. Their business kept them busy, traveling, sneaking around. Thankfully they had enough law enforcement in their back pocket to keep them out of the hot seat, but still. Laney always worried something would happen. There were worse fates than being arrested.

"We're all fine." Braden took the ornament from her and waited until she turned her attention toward him. "I'm asking about you. Are you still receiving threats? I'd hoped after Shane—"

"Stop worrying about me."

She didn't want to talk about her emails or Shane. Ryker had taken it upon himself to…handle the problem of Shane when he'd attempted to abduct Laney from in front of her home in Beacon Hill. Shane had been the bane of her family's existence for years, but he'd crossed the line when he'd harassed Braden's wife, Zara. When he'd tried to grab Laney, Ryker had had enough.

And Laney knew the way Ryker had managed the situation had been an issue between him and Braden. Since Braden had taken over the family business after their father passed, he'd been adamant about going legitimate, and that included how they took care of their enemies. Ryker insisted that ending their old practices so suddenly would make them look weak and invite retribution.

Laney was still unsure what happened to her ex, but she was fine about being kept in the dark regarding that.

"Why don't you get back home to your bride?" Laney suggested. "It's late. I'm just going to sit here and tear up a little over Mom's things."

Braden looked as if he wanted to say more. That intense stare could make even the most seasoned criminal break, but Laney wasn't caving. She'd grown up around strong-willed alphas her entire life. Not much fazed her.

"If you have any issues, you call me or Ryker immediately."

Laney nodded, though if she had an issue she'd deal with it herself. She wasn't a helpless female.

Once she hugged her loving, overprotective brother good-night, she reset her alarm and glanced around at the mess. The tree sat completely naked in the corner near the fireplace where she always put it. She wasn't even sure at this point if she had any working lights. She tried to buy new ones each year, but, well, this year had been a bit exceptional and her mind had been elsewhere.

Laney found the box with her garland and decided to work on the staircase. That would be simple enough and keep her mind occupied for a few minutes.

She'd barely started when her thoughts drifted to Ryker. There was always a level of fear anytime she knew he was working. But the not knowing was frustrating. She knew the lead he was working on, she'd supplied him with the intel, but she didn't like how he insisted on going out alone. He always stayed just detached enough to be in the know but keep to himself. Damn frustrating man.

Laney carefully wrapped the banister, fluffing the greenery as she went. This time next year she'd be playing Santa and buying the baby's first Christmas things— tacky bibs and ridiculous ornaments would be welcome here.

What would her world be like with a child? Laney smiled. As scared as she was to tell her brothers, as worried as she was about what this meant for her and Ryker, there was no way Laney would change one single thing about Miami. This baby would never question how much he or she was loved, and the first person to call this pregnancy a mistake would be throat punched.

The thought of Ryker holding a baby was nearly

laughable. She'd never seen his softer side, though she knew he had one. He cared for her, even if he opted to show it in Neanderthal-type ways.

Those whispered words before he left kept playing through her mind. She wished he'd stayed so they could talk, but he was prone to run rather than discuss his feelings. Well, he couldn't hide from her forever. Eventually they had to talk about the future and their baby.

Laney's cell chimed from the living room. She hurried down the stairs and carefully maneuvered the minefield of boxes. She found her phone on the coffee table next to a wreath that was in desperate need of fluffing. Because of the time of night, she figured the text would be important.

And she was right.

Ryker's name lit up her screen, and she swiped her phone to read the message.

Nothing new tonight. Anything come through on your end?

Work. It was always work with him. A sliver of disappointment speared through her as she replied.

Nothing. I'll keep you posted.

Her thumb hovered over the Send button. She wanted to make this more personal. She wanted to say…something. But Ryker was all work. What would he say if she asked personal questions or called him out on what he'd confessed to her earlier? Could he talk about his feelings when he wasn't looking her in the face? She understood that. She totally got how people were more apt to open up when they could hide behind an electronic device.

She hit Send but immediately started typing another message.

Earlier when you said you think about me, why were you angry about it?

Laney sent the message before she could change her mind. She wanted to know. She deserved to know, but the screen seemed to mock her as no reply came. She waited several minutes, but still nothing.

Fine. She wasn't going to beg. Yes, she would give anything to get inside that head of his, but she didn't want to have to beat the information out of him.

The second she laid her phone down, it chimed once again. Laney stared at the screen. She almost didn't want to read the message, but she hadn't been raised to give into any fear.

Because it isn't right.

Laney resisted the urge to roll her eyes as she contemplated her reply. There was so much to be said, it was too much to text and should be said face-to-face.

But he wasn't completely closing her out, so she went for it.

Whatever you feel can't be helped. Why fight it?

Laney jumped when her phone rang. The cell bounced from her hand and onto the sofa, hit a box and landed on the floor. She snatched it up, thankful the screen wasn't cracked, and she was a bit surprised to see Ryker's name.

"I didn't think you'd actually talk to me," she answered.

"You wouldn't leave me alone until I did."

Laney smiled. Just that gruff tone had her nerves calming. Ryker could always make her feel safe, at ease. Even though they argued and got on each other's nerves, he was her comfort zone. Banter was their normal. Normal was so vanilla. What she and Ryker had, well...that was more Rocky Road.

"Where are you now?" she asked, scooting a box over and taking a seat on her couch.

"Hotel."

"Plenty of time to talk, then."

Ryker's heavy sigh resounded through the line. "I'm not in a chatty mood."

"Have you ever been?"

"What do you think?"

Laney toed the disorderly wreath aside and propped her socked feet on the coffee table. "Maybe it's time you stop fighting whatever you're feeling and just go with it."

The laugh that escaped him was void of any humor. "Life isn't that easy."

"It's your life, isn't it? Make it that easy."

"You think I enjoy pushing my level of self-control?" he asked, his voice gravelly, as if fighting back anger. "I have a responsibility to your brothers. I have a responsibility to you." He let out a deep sigh. "To our baby."

Laney's heart clenched. Closing her eyes, she dropped her head back on the cushion and focused on not botching this. Ryker was so much more to her than she could even put into words, but he may never comprehend that.

"You have a responsibility to yourself," she said softly. "You owe my family nothing. I know you think you—"

"I owe your family everything. And I've betrayed them."

His last words came out on a strangled breath. Laney stilled. Did he honestly believe that? Was he that torn up over the baby that he truly felt he'd gone against her brothers? Why did everything have to come back to his sense of loyalty to her family? They trusted him, they knew him better than anyone else and they might be angry, but they would still love him.

Tears pricked her eyes, and she cursed her stupid pregnancy hormones. Tears had no place here. She was fighting for what she wanted, what Ryker wanted. Hell, what they deserved.

"If that's how you feel, then there's nothing I can say. If you don't want anyone to know this baby is yours, we don't have to say anything. I can just say I'm not involved with the father and not tell my brothers any name at all." Though it would kill her. Pain like nothing before speared through her at the thought of Ryker not being involved. "I can't make you want—"

"That's the whole problem," he yelled. "I want, damn it. Too much. But I'll never turn my back on you or this baby."

Laney picked at the hem of her T-shirt and swallowed a lump of remorse. "Right. Responsibilities."

"Laney—"

"It's late. I'll let you go."

She ended the call, dropping the phone into her lap as she battled back tears. Why did he have to be so noble, yet so ignorant at the same time? Why did he feel that he had to sacrifice his own happiness in order to fulfill

some past debt? Ryker had more than proved himself to
this family.

At least he hadn't agreed to being left out of the
baby's life. That would've gutted her. But he still only
saw her as a responsibility, and Laney feared she'd never
be more in his life.

Four

"We need to get inside that house."

Braden nodded in agreement. "How soon can you get back? I don't want them moving that trunk."

Ryker leaned back on the leather sofa in Braden's study. He'd left New York after staying an extra day longer than planned, and had driven straight to Braden's house. He hadn't called or texted Laney after their talk on the phone. He'd revealed too much, she'd gotten too close to the raw emotions…emotions he feared he couldn't hide forever.

Damn it. He hadn't even been aware of suppressing them, so how the hell did he continue to hide them?

"I can go as soon as I get the blueprint."

Braden came to his feet. "Great. Laney is due here anytime."

The blueprint was a pathetic excuse to see her again.

He could've gotten it the other day when she offered, she could've also emailed it. But, he wanted to see her, touch her, consume her. But reality was cold and harsh. He'd had her once, and that would have to stay with him forever because he couldn't let his guard down again.

He'd not only betrayed Braden and Mac by slashing right through their trust, but he'd let Laney down, as well. He should've had more control in Miami, should've walked her to her room and kept going once he knew she was safe. How could he have let his all-consuming need for her change their entire lives?

"Ryker?"

Jerking his attention back to Braden, Ryker stood. "Lost in thought. What were you saying?"

"Laney just pulled in."

Ryker glanced to the monitors and saw Laney stepping from her car. While it had stopped snowing, the ground was blanketed in several inches. Braden's drive and walk had been cleared though.

He tried not to watch as she pulled her coat tighter around her waist or how her long, dark hair blew in the breeze. He didn't have to concentrate too hard to still feel that hair over his body. Ryker clenched his fists and ordered himself to get control before she stepped inside. This would be the first time the three of them would be together since he'd found out about the pregnancy. He couldn't give anything away. He couldn't—

On the screen, Laney slipped and went down. Ryker tore out of the study, down the hall and through the foyer. He whipped open the door, oblivious to the wind and the bitter air. Laney had a gloved hand on the bumper of her car and was pushing herself up.

"Stop." Ryker slid his arms around her waist. "Lean into me."

Laney pushed her hair away from her face and looked up at him. "I'm fine. Embarrassed, but fine."

Ryker didn't let her go as she came fully to her feet.

"Is she okay?"

Ryker glanced over his shoulder to Braden who was coming toward them. "I think so."

Laney tried to push off Ryker, but winced. "Okay. Just give me a second."

His hands flattened over her stomach as his heart sank. "Laney?"

Her eyes held his. "It's my ankle. Just sore. I'm okay."

How did she know? Could she be sure the baby was okay? Ryker didn't know how hard she fell. Hell, he didn't know anything about pregnancies or babies, but seeing her go down had nearly stopped his heart.

Scooping her up in his arms, and careful to avoid random ice patches, he stalked past Braden and into the house. Zara rushed in from the kitchen, her dark hair flying around her shoulders.

"What happened? Laney?"

"I'm okay." Laney waved a hand. "Just slipped outside and my ankle is sore. Ryker is being overbearing as usual."

Considering he'd been that way with her for years, this wasn't out of the ordinary. He didn't give a damn if it was. Seeing Laney go down like that had ripped something open inside him. In the brief seconds it took him to get outside, all he could think of was their baby. How the hell was he going to handle parenting?

"I'll get some ice," Zara told them.

Ryker gently laid Laney on the chaise in the formal

living room. Her hand slid against the side of his neck as she let go. Even though she had gloves on, just that simple touch took him back to Miami when she'd—

No. That was then. A mistake. He couldn't live in the past. He'd vowed to move on and that's exactly what he had to do if he wanted to get their intimacy out of his life.

Unfortunately, Laney had imbedded herself into his soul…and he thought he'd sold that to the devil a long time ago.

But he felt her. When she looked at him, he swore he felt her. That delicate touch, the tender gaze. She was hurting now, and he needed to focus.

"I'll call our doctor," Ryker stated.

Laney immediately started to shake her head. "I just went down wrong. I'm fine. I didn't fall hard."

"Let's get your boot off and look at your ankle." Braden went to unzip her boot. "Can you move it at all?"

She wiggled her foot, and Ryker watched her face for any sign of discomfort. When her bright eyes flashed up to his, he had to tell himself not to look away. She could draw him in so easily…and she knew the power she possessed.

"It's a little swollen," Braden commented. "I'd say you're fine. Just stay off it for a while."

Laney smirked. Freakin' smirked at him like a child who'd been playing parents against each other. Ryker narrowed his eyes. "I'm calling the doctor anyway just to be safe."

Before he could slide his cell from his pocket, Laney laid a hand on his wrist. "I'm fine." Her eyes bore into his, completely serious now. "I promise. I'd know if I needed to be seen."

She didn't look away, her grip tightened. Ryker blew

out a breath he wasn't aware he'd been holding. Of course she would get a doctor here if she thought she needed one. Laney loved this baby and wouldn't make poor choices. Still, for his peace of mind, he'd feel better if she was seen.

"Relax," she whispered, her eyes darting toward her brother.

Yeah. Relax.

Ryker took a step back and glanced down at her ankle. He needed to get a grip. Being cautious and protective was one thing, but acting like a hovering boyfriend was—

Seriously? How had that word even popped into his head? He wasn't her damn boyfriend. This wasn't junior high. But she was right. If he didn't get a grip, Braden would wonder what was going on, and that wasn't a topic he wanted to dive headfirst into right now.

"Here you go." Zara came back in and placed an ice pack wrapped in a towel over Laney's ankle. "Let's put a pillow under you to keep it propped up."

Ryker stayed back as Braden and Zara got Laney situated. He wanted to scoop her up and take her back to his house where he could take care of her. He wanted her tucked away behind his state-of-the-art security system where she'd be safe at all times. But none of that was possible. She'd never be at his house on personal terms. He'd never see her in his bed.

Ryker reached into his pocket, his fingertips brushing over the penny. The reminder he wasn't cut out for family life.

"Do you feel like working?" Braden asked. "I hate to ask, but time is of the essence."

Laney shifted on the sofa. "I can work. My laptop is

out in the car, though. I was walking to the passenger side to get it when I fell."

"I'll get it."

Ryker needed more cool air. He needed to get his heart rate back to normal and to chill out. Laney had had to talk him down, and that had never happened. Damn it.

She may not want a doctor, but one thing was certain. When they left here, he'd be driving her. Whether they went to her house or his, that was her choice, but they'd be leaving together.

Laney concentrated on digging up the layout of the house Ryker needed to get into. Her ankle throbbed more than she wanted to admit, but she was absolutely certain nothing else was hurt. The baby was fine. If she even thought for a second that something could be wrong, she'd have a doctor here. But she honestly hadn't fallen that hard, just turned her ankle on the sliver of ice she hadn't seen.

Zara and Braden were in the study. Her brother had told her to yell when she found something because he was helping his wife work on finalizing the company party.

Laney's sister-in-law was a top-notch events coordinator and in high demand. The way Braden supported her business was adorable. He was proud of his wife, and their love was evident whenever they were around each other.

The miscarriage they'd suffered a few months ago had only forged their bond even deeper. But Laney still couldn't bring herself to tell them about her own condition.

"Will you stop brooding?" Laney's fingers flew over the keys, but Ryker's presence was wearing on her nerves.

"I'm waiting."

She glanced over to him and raised her brows. "You're leaning in the corner with your arms crossed, and you've been staring for twenty minutes. That's brooding. I can actually hear your frustration."

When he pushed from the wall and strode over to her, Laney realized she'd poked the bear. Fine. At least he was showing emotion.

Ryker loomed over her, hands on his narrow hips. "How much longer until you have something?"

"I'm downloading the blueprints now."

"Good. Then we're leaving."

Laney jerked back. "Excuse me?"

He leaned down, pinning her with those coal-black eyes. "You heard me. I'm driving. The destination is up to you."

O-kay. The clenched jaw and the no-nonsense tone told her he wasn't giving her an option.

"Fine. We're going to my house. I have things I need to get done."

Ryker shoved his hands in his pockets. "Not with that ankle. You're relaxing, and if I even think you're trying to put weight on it, I'll have the doctor at your house so fast you won't know what hit you."

Laney believed him. He didn't take chances with her on a good day, but add in a pregnancy and a fall, and Ryker was dead serious.

"Oh, don't worry." She offered him her sweetest smile. "I plan on letting you do all the work."

Poor guy. He had no idea he was about to be covered head to toe in glittery garland, lights and delicate glass ornaments. She'd most certainly have her phone at the ready to snap some pictures of Ryker decorating her house.

"Oh, here we go." She glanced back at her screen, surveyed the pages that had downloaded and quickly emailed them to Braden and Ryker. "All done."

Ryker stalked from the room. There was no other word to describe his movements. He was angry, most likely with himself, or maybe with her. Whatever. He was about to be doused in Christmas happiness. He wanted to order her around and demand he leave with her? Fine.

Laney hesitated for a second but quickly pulled up her emails. Nothing new on the property in Southie. She'd had some contractors survey the building so she could get some quotes. After she signed the paperwork next week, the place would officially be hers and she could get to work. She seriously wanted the place open by spring so kids could come and play when the weather got nicer.

Opening the community center in Ryker's old neighborhood was perfect. She couldn't wait to have children filling the place. Children who may not have an exemplary home life and just needed a break.

Laney wondered where Ryker would be today if someone had intervened and helped him earlier than her father had. Would he still be part of their lives? Would he still be as hard, as jaded as he was now? He'd made it a point to be her personal security detail from the time she was a teenager. Was that because no one had protected him?

Laney's heart clenched. Had his worry for her led to whatever happened to her ex?

No. She wouldn't believe that Ryker would do anything to him beyond a few harassing calls and texts. Ryker could be over the top at times when it came to people he cared about, but she truly hoped he hadn't done anything rash.

Laney swallowed as she closed her laptop. Ryker cared about her. Beyond their intense night together, he'd admitted as much...and he didn't mean the sibling type of caring, either.

Ryker may think he'd been keeping her safe, but she always had his back, too. She held the reins with the intel coming in, and she chose what to feed him and what to keep to herself.

Laney would be even more diligent now that he was going to be a father. There might be times she made sure he didn't get a case because of the danger it posed to him, and she'd deal with the backlash from her brothers. Ryker needed someone to look after him; he was long overdue for it, actually. And Laney was just the woman for the job.

Five

The second Ryker stepped into Laney's house, he froze. He'd been duped. He glanced at her, only to see a smirk on her beautiful face. Now she mocked him.

Why did he find himself so attracted to her again? Oh, yeah. She was sexy as hell, and she took charge. A perfectly lethal combination to his senses. If he were ever considering a relationship, those were the qualities he'd look for. But a relationship with Laney was not only risky, it was suicide.

"Don't even tell me I'm decorating."

Laney leaned on him because she wouldn't let him carry her, yet she was limping slightly. Stubborn woman.

"I can do it, but you'll just get all grouchy and make me sit down."

Ryker reset her alarm system, still wishing he'd ignored her request and gone to his own house. After escorting her over to her sofa with an attached chaise, he got her settled and pulled off her boots. He grabbed one of her fluffy yellow throw pillows and set it beneath her ankle.

"Still sore?" he asked, glancing down at her, trying to ignore how perfect she looked all laid out.

"It's fine."

Ryker crossed his arms over his chest and sighed. "You've said that at least five times since it happened, which means it's anything but fine."

Laney tipped her head back on the cushion, her hair falling around her shoulders. Try as he might, he couldn't help but recall how all those strands felt on his bare skin. A memory he prayed never diminished. He needed that to keep him going, especially since he'd never have her again.

"Stop hovering. My ankle is fine, the baby is fine." She laced her fingers over her abdomen. "Do you want to put the lights on the tree or would you prefer to decorate the mantel?"

Ryker narrowed his eyes. Testing his patience was a surefire way to get him to take her back to his house. Did he look like a damn interior designer?

"Maybe you didn't notice, but I don't do Christmas."

"I always buy you a gift. In fact, you're the first person I buy for."

Yeah, and he'd kept every single one of them. He always felt like a fool for not buying her something, but what would he get her? What was an appropriate gift for a woman he wanted but couldn't have? So he never did gifts...for anyone.

"You don't have to buy me gifts," he growled. He'd rather put up lights than get into this uncomfortable topic.

Laney shifted on the chaise and patted the spot beside her. "You're staring down at me like I'm a bug on your shoe. So, either sit down, get to work or leave."

Ryker loved how she always spoke her mind. Except when she kept revealing her feelings for him. Nothing good could come from her making an impossible situation even more difficult.

And if he sat next to her, he'd want to touch her. Touching would lead to what they both truly wanted, and he refused to betray this family again by giving into his selfish desires.

Ryker turned and grabbed a box. "What's in here?"

From the corner of his eye, he saw Laney's shoulders fall, her eyes close. He'd hurt her. He couldn't sit close to her. Didn't she get that? She had to understand this wasn't about them. There was so much more to it than just a man and a woman who were attracted to each other. So he'd have to keep his distance...as much as possible, no matter how much he wanted her.

"That's the ornaments," she told him. "I have a bag of lights I just purchased. It's on the steps. There's also a bag from All Seasons there, but be careful because I just bought the cutest Nutcracker there."

Fine. He'd put the damn lights on the tree. He'd decorate her house to put a smile on her face. He knew full well how much Laney loved Christmas. She used to go to her parents' house, which was now Braden and Zara's, and cook an elaborate dinner on Christmas Eve. She'd pass out gifts she'd bought and wrapped in thick, sparkly paper. Most likely she'd hand tied her own bows, too. Laney's face would light up as she sat and watched her family open their gifts. Ryker was always so mesmerized, so humbled he got to experience Christmas with them.

Damn it. They were his family. The only family he'd truly considered his own—the only one that mattered.

He'd just reached the steps and spotted the bag when Laney's soft voice stopped him.

"I know you don't want to be here."

Ryker glanced over his shoulder. Those bright green eyes locked him in place from across the room.

"I never said that."

Smiling, she said, "You didn't have to. You regret sleeping with me. Probably feel trapped because I'm pregnant. And I'm positive you think you betrayed my brothers. But please, don't patronize me or pity me. I'm fine on my own, Ryker."

When she held her ground and didn't glance away, he ignored the bag and started back toward Laney. She was a strong woman, what man wouldn't find that a complete turn on? She was everything he'd want in a woman, but she was the little sister of his employers, his best friends. She was off limits. And he'd ignored that unwritten rule.

Taking a seat on the edge of the chaise, he faced her. "I don't regret sleeping with you. I've tried, but I can't even lie to myself."

She reached out, tracing his scarred knuckles with her fingertip. "That's something, at least."

"I don't feel trapped," he went on. "I feel sorry for you, for this baby. I know nothing, Laney. The most impressionable years of my childhood were spent in hell. I couldn't begin to tell you what a baby needs. I don't even know how to help you adjust to this. I'm not made to be in a relationship or to be a parent. But that doesn't mean I'm turning my back on you guys. It just means…"

Ryker shook his head and turned away so he didn't have to look her in the eye. Apparently she was the stronger of the two. "It means you deserve better, and this is what you've got."

He barely heard her shift before her fingers threaded through his hair. "There's nobody better than you, Ryker. You're a fighter, you're noble and you're loyal. I know you'd do anything to keep me and this baby safe. What makes you think I'm so unlucky?"

Reaching up, he gripped her wrist, but didn't pull her hand away as he turned to meet her questioning gaze. "Because you deserve a man you can share your life with. You're the type who wants a family, who wants that big Christmas morning celebration with chaos and Santa stories. I can't give you that."

Laney smoothed his hair from his forehead. He should stop her. He should remove her hand, but he was such a selfish bastard. One more touch. He just needed one more and then he'd get up.

"Have I asked you for anything? You're already family. Just because we're having a baby doesn't mean you have to marry me."

Just the thought of marriage had him trembling. He traveled too much, took too many risks to bring a wife into the mix.

Laney's hand fell to her lap. "I didn't realize you were so put off by the thought of marriage. Glad I didn't propose."

She'd tried to make light of the situation, but the hurt in her tone gave her away.

"Laney—"

"So, if you want to bring me that sack of lights, I can

get them out of the boxes, and you can put them on the tree."

He stared at her another minute, to which her response was to stare right back, as if daring him to turn the topic back around. Ryker didn't necessarily want to get into a verbal sparring match with her, so he nodded and went to get the bag.

He'd thought Christmas decorating was torture, but seeing Laney hurt, knowing he'd caused her feelings to be crushed, was even worse. He was going to have to learn how to make her smile again or...what? It wasn't as if he could remove himself from her life. He worked for her family, and she was having his baby.

For once in his life, Ryker had no idea what the hell to do. He'd lived on the streets, he'd fought for his next meal and he'd taken risks that not even Mac or Braden knew about. But the shaky ground he stood on with Laney was the scariest thing he'd ever had to face.

Laney wasn't sure what was more amusing, Ryker cursing at the tangle of lights that had somehow wrapped itself around his shoulders, or Spike and Rapture continually getting into the tree and swatting at Ryker's hand.

Poor cats. They thought Ryker wanted to play each time he reached for another branch. Most of the time her cats kept to themselves, ignored her completely. But the excitement of the tree and the boxes had brought them out of hiding.

Laney realized she had completely forgotten about the pain in her ankle. The entertainment in her living room was more than enough to keep her distracted.

But part of her couldn't help but drift to the "what-if" state. The scenario right now with Ryker decorating,

Laney pregnant, resting on the chaise, the fire roaring and the cats playing, it was like a scene from a Christmas card.

Laney couldn't lie to herself. She wanted that Christmas card. She wanted to have a family like the one she'd grown up in. The O'Sheas were Irish—they knew how to do family gatherings. She had always dreamed of having her own home, having a husband and children. She'd never seen her future any differently.

Perhaps she was going about her plan in the wrong order, but she still had every hope of having children and a husband.

So, how would Ryker fit into this mix? He wasn't exactly the type of man she'd envisioned when she'd been doing her daydreaming. She'd never thought of being with a man who had scarred knuckles, tattoos, constant scruff along his jawline and an attitude that matched that of her cocky brothers.

Still, Ryker was absolutely everything that got her excited. He turned her on and made her want more—and not just physically. Ryker always made her feel safe, even if he drove her out of her mind.

Perhaps that's why she was so drawn to him. He didn't back down, he didn't care what her last name was and he matched her wits.

Laney stared across the room as Ryker reached toward the top of the tree for the last section of lights. So what if she was admiring the way his T-shirt rode up when he reached or the way his worn jeans covered his backside.

"Why are you staring?"

Laney blinked, realizing Ryker had glanced over his shoulder. Oops. Oh, well, it wouldn't be the last time she'd be caught ogling.

"I've never had a hotter decorator," she told him with a smile. "Next you can start on the ornaments."

Ryker turned. Hands propped on his hips, he shook his head. "This isn't going to work. Whatever is in your mind, get it out."

Laney shifted on the chaise to prop her elbow on the arm. Resting her chin in her hand, she raised her brows. "I don't know what you're talking about."

"The innocent act also doesn't work on me."

Laney laughed. "No? Offering to strip my clothes seemed to work."

Ryker's stony expression told her he didn't find her nearly as amusing as she found herself.

"Listen, we're going to have to learn to get along," she told him. "We can't always be griping at each other. You need to relax."

"Relax? You think I'll ever relax, especially now that you're having my child?"

Laney shrugged. "Shouldn't I be the one freaking out? I mean, I'm carrying the baby."

Ryker raked a hand over his jaw, the bristling of his stubble against his palm doing nothing to douse the desire she had for him. She recalled exactly what the coarse hair felt like on her heated skin. She'd give anything to feel it all over again.

"Are you that worried about my brothers?" she asked. "I mean, once they find out about the baby, they'll get used to the idea of us being together."

"We aren't together."

Laney met his dark gaze. "We could be."

Laying it all out there was ridiculous. Her hint was about as subtle as a two-by-four to the head, but she wanted him to see that they could at least try to be more.

"No, we can't." Glancing around the room, he located a box marked Ornaments and pulled off the lid. "You know why and I'm not going to discuss this every time we're together. I already told you I'd support you and our baby."

"I don't want your money." Laney swung her legs over the side of the chaise and pushed off, using the arm of the sofa for support. "I want you to stop dancing around this attraction. We already know we're compatible between the sheets."

"Sit down before you hurt yourself." In three strides he'd reached her and was ushering her back down. "I hope you don't care how the ornaments are put up because I've never done this before."

Laney didn't budge, but it was difficult to hold her ground when he was pushing her and she was putting her weight on one foot.

"Why are you so stubborn?" she demanded, then waited until he looked her in the eyes. "Seriously. Can't you just tell me why you won't even consider giving this a chance?"

His fingers curled around her shoulders. "Because you see something in me, in us, that isn't there."

"I see potential. I see a man who wants something and never goes after it. He's too busy working his ass off for everyone around him."

The muscles in his jaw clenched. "That's enough, Laney."

"Is it?" she threw back. "Because I don't think it's near enough. I think you need someone to tell you just what the—"

His mouth slammed onto hers. For a split second she was stunned, then she was thrilled. Finally. He was finally taking what he wanted.

Those hands moved from her shoulders at once. One went to the small of her back, pulling her closer to his body. The other crept up beneath her hair, fisting it and jerking her head just where he wanted it.

Laney held on to his biceps to steady herself. A full-on attack like this required a bit of warning. She supposed her warning had been his intense gaze, the way he stalked across the room toward her. The way he'd torn her dress weeks ago.

Ryker broke the kiss, his forehead resting against hers. "You have to stop."

Excuse me? "You kissed me."

"To shut you up," he growled. "I can't keep fighting this with you. You push and push until I snap."

"Maybe I push so you can see what it is you're missing."

Ryker pulled in a deep breath and took a step back. His arms dropped to his sides. "Believe me, I know what I'm missing."

If she'd ever met a more frustrating man, she couldn't recall. "What would you do if I quit pushing?" she countered. "Maybe one day I'll give up, move on. What would you do then?"

Six

Ryker shoved his hand in his pockets, a futile attempt at reaching for her. There was nothing he wanted more than to take her and rip those clothes off and make use of that sofa.

The penny in his pocket mocked him, reminding him of where he came from, of who he actually was. If he were a better man, a man who could offer Laney and their baby something of worth, he wouldn't think twice about taking her up on her offer.

"I won't wait on you forever," she whispered. "I feel like I've already waited most of my life. We had one night and you flipped out. And that was before you found out about the baby."

Ryker didn't know what to say. He didn't do feelings, and he sure as hell didn't discuss them. Laney was right, though. He'd flipped out after their night together.

Never in his life had he ever felt something so perfect—
he didn't deserve perfect. In the midst of betraying the
only family he'd ever loved, he'd found a dose of happiness he never knew he was longing for.

"I think we're done here." Laney eased herself back
onto the chaise. Clearly she'd taken his silence as rejec-
tion. "I'm tired. Set the alarm on your way out."

"You think I'd leave when you're this upset?"

Laney's bright green eyes misted. "I'm not upset. I'm
exhausted. I've beat my head against the proverbial wall
for too long, and now I have a child who needs my attention. I have to look out for myself now, and if you
can't see what we could be, then we have nothing left
to discuss."

Getting shut out was not what he wanted, damn it,
but he couldn't let himself in, either. There was no right
answer, but there was an answer that would keep Laney
and their baby safe.

"We need to tell Mac and Braden soon." Ryker ignored the pain in his chest. Pain was just a by-product
of doing the right thing for those he cared about. "I'll do
anything for you and our baby, Laney, but I can't be that
perfect man in your life. You know why."

She kept her focus on her lap where her hands were
folded. "I know you're a coward, so maybe you're not
the man I want."

Her harsh words gutted him. The idea of her being
with anyone else made him want to hit the faceless bastard. How could Ryker let her go so easily?

Because she was an O'Shea. Her father had taken
Ryker in when he'd been on the verge of going down a
path of complete destruction. Respecting Patrick, keeping his relationships with Mac and Braden, that's what

Ryker needed to do. He'd built his entire life around working for them, taking risks to keep them safe and going through hell in keeping his distance from Laney.

He'd failed. His penance would be to let her go.

"Let me at least help you to—"

"I don't need your help." Laney held up a hand, her lips thinned in anger, though her eyes still held unshed tears. "Since you won't take a chance, then I have nothing left to say to you right now. I'll let you know when my doctor's appointment is, and I'll fill you in on work. Other than that, we're done."

Swallowing, Ryker nodded. "I'm going back to New York since you got me the blueprints of the DeLuca property. I don't know when I'll be back, but shouldn't be more than a couple of days."

When she said nothing, Ryker moved around the coffee table and the storage boxes. He grabbed his coat off the hook by the front door and had just jerked the leather over his shoulders when her soft voice stopped him.

"Be careful."

With his back to her, Ryker closed his eyes.

"I may be angry with you, but I still care and I want you safe," she went on. "Your baby is counting on you to be here."

His baby. Words he never thought would come to mean so much to him.

"I can take care of myself." He opened the door and typed in the alarm code.

He thought he heard her mutter, "That's what scares me," before he closed the door, but he didn't stop to ask. The bitter cold whipped around him. Ryker pulled his jacket tighter around his shoulders and made his way off her porch and toward his SUV. Walking away from

Laney was the hardest thing he'd ever done. Before Miami, he'd always thought not knowing what being intimate with her felt like was the worst thing, but he'd been wrong. Because now he knew. Now he was fully aware of how perfect they were, how compatible they were. Now he had to live with the knowledge that he'd never have something that amazing in his life.

As Ryker slid behind the wheel of his car, he cursed himself. In the long run, this was the right answer. He'd been teetering on the wrong side of the law for so long, and he should finally feel good about a decision he was making.

So why did he feel like hell?

"It's a trap." Laney gripped her phone and tried not to panic as she left Ryker a voicemail. The third in as many hours. "Don't go inside. It's all been a setup."

She stood in Braden's office, staring out the massive wall of windows that overlooked a snow-blanketed backyard. She'd come here after her first call and several texts had gone unanswered. It was late, too late to be worrying about Ryker and this damn job. She should be at home asleep. Ryker should be safe in his hotel room. But she'd been given intel that the DeLuca home was going to be empty around eight in the evening, and Ryker had been given the green light to go in, check the trunk in the basement and get out before they arrived back sometime around midnight.

It was now one in the morning, and nobody had heard a word.

"Find out something, damn it." Braden's frustration level was just as high as hers as he shouted into his cell. "Call me back."

Laney turned to face her brother. "Anything?"

"I called one of our FBI guys in that area, and he's looking into where Ryker is."

Which meant they still knew nothing. Laney tamped down her fear because Ryker had been in sticky situations before. For years she worried each time he went out, but he'd always come back. On occasion he'd dodge the topic of why he had new scrapes or bruises, or a run-in with the law, but he always returned.

All Laney could think of was how they'd left things last night. Why had she told him that she was done? If he came back right now and told her he wanted to give things a shot, she'd be right there with him. He was it for her.

Laney smoothed her hand down the front of her tunic and over her flat stomach. She needed to remain calm for the baby. Ryker was okay...he had to be.

"He'll be fine," Braden assured her. "It's Ryker. You know he's probably somewhere laying low. Most likely he's hiding in that house with his phone on silent and dodging the DeLucas. You know he loves a challenge."

Laney jerked the leather chair from behind the desk and sank into it. "You're not helping. It's all my fault for giving him that information."

"Laney, you were going on a lead. That's all."

Exhaustion had long since set in. She hadn't slept well after Ryker had left last night. Then today she'd been searching for the root of her troublesome emails that had been sent a couple months ago when she'd gotten another bit of information on the DeLuca property. She'd instantly noticed something was wrong when the chatter turned to humorous banter about a setup. She'd almost gotten sick. After her texts to Ryker went unanswered, she called. And called.

She hadn't suffered much morning sickness yet, but the constant state of I-need-a-nap was ever-present. This situation with the DeLucas wasn't helping. All the worrying, all the fear. She wanted to believe the best because she wasn't sure she could handle it if Ryker got hurt...or worse.

Laney crossed her arms on the desk, making them a pillow for her head. Strong hands came to rub her shoulders.

"Relax," Braden told her. "Any minute he'll walk through the door and get angry because you're worrying."

Yeah, that was so like Ryker. She wished for that scenario more than anything.

"I swear, when you two aren't at each other's throats, you're both worrywarts."

Laney couldn't respond. She was too busy enjoying the massage and trying to wrap her mind around how she'd survive if something happened to Ryker.

Oh, she'd live and get along, but she'd be empty. Her child would be fatherless. She couldn't imagine anything scarier. Ryker had been in her life for so long, she truly didn't know how to exist without him.

When Braden's cell chimed, Laney jerked her head up and turned to stare as he answered.

"Yeah?"

Her brother's hard jaw, set mouth and grip on the phone weren't helping her nerves, but that was just typical Braden. As head of the family now, he was all business, all the time. Mac, their more carefree brother, was still down in Miami with his fiancée, Jenna. Those two had danced around their attraction for years…which reminded Laney of another stubborn couple she knew.

"Where is he now?"

Laney jerked to her feet, hanging on each and every word, watching to see if Braden's expression changed. Was Ryker okay? She wanted answers. Right. Now.

"I'll be waiting."

Braden pocketed his phone. "He's fine," he assured her. "But he was arrested. After some strings were pulled in the right direction, my contact with the Bureau managed to get him released. Ryker is being escorted by my acquaintance. I'm going to meet them just outside the city in a few hours."

Laney gripped the desk for support. "I'm going with you."

Braden put a hand on her arm. "You're going home. He's fine and it's late."

When she started to protest, Braden shook his head. "No, Laney. I don't know what's gotten into you. This is Ryker. You know he's fine. He'll be annoying you by morning, I'm sure."

What had gotten into her? Well, the father of her baby had been arrested, though the charges wouldn't stick because of their connections. He'd been set up in a trap that could've gone so much worse than what it had been.

How could she do this? How could she keep letting herself get all worked up over a man who kept pushing her away?

Finally Laney nodded. "Will you text me once you see him? Just to let me know he's really okay?"

After she grabbed her purse and keys, Braden kissed her cheek. "I will. Now go home and get some sleep."

Laney wouldn't sleep until she knew for sure. And

a text from Braden wasn't good enough. She wanted to see with her own eyes.

As she let herself out of her childhood home in Beacon Hill, Laney knew just where to go.

Seven

The last thirty-six hours had been a bitch. Ryker wanted nothing more than to get into his home and crawl between the sheets of his king-size bed. So much could've gone wrong in New York, but he refused to dwell on that. All he could concentrate on was the fact that he'd failed. One more dead end.

No scrolls. He hadn't even gotten to the mysterious damn trunk in the basement before he'd been caught off guard and cuffed.

Punching in his security code, Ryker let himself in. The sun was bright and promising a new day…and he was thankful for thick blinds. He hadn't slept since he left Boston. He sure as hell hadn't been able to relax when he'd been taken into custody. Not that he'd been worried. This wasn't his first run-in with the law, but he didn't have time for all this nonsense.

As soon as he stepped through his door and closed
it behind his back, Ryker took in the sight before him.
Without turning, he reached over his shoulder and reset
the alarm. He wasn't about to take his eyes off the sleeping beauty perfectly placed on his leather sofa.

Laney wasn't quite lying down. She had her feet
curled up to the side, her hands were tucked under her
face, which rested on the arm of the couch. She looked
so fragile, so small. But he knew she was neither. There
was a vibrancy, a strength in her that terrified him. She
feared nothing. He'd never found a woman who was willing to verbally spar with him like Laney. She wasn't
afraid to throw back anything he dished out. She was
absolutely perfect.

And she was the most beautiful sight he'd seen in
days.

Ryker released the grip on his bag until it thunked
onto the hardwood floor. He shed his coat and hung it up.
She still didn't stir. Pregnancy was taking its toll on her.
It wasn't like his Laney to be tired all the time.

Ryker froze. *His Laney?* Not in this lifetime. She'd
never be completely his. But he was on a slippery slope
and wasn't going to be able to hold on much longer. He'd
told her before he was selfish, he'd proved that in Miami.
But there was going to come a point when he wouldn't
be able to turn her away.

Laney stirred, blinked until she focused on him, then
jerked awake. The tousled hair, the slight crease on her
cheek from where she'd lain, the flawless face void of
any makeup staring back at him…maybe that time had
come.

He started forward as Laney swung her legs off the
side of the couch and stood. "I'm sorry. I didn't mean to

fall asleep," she stated, tugging her long shirt in place over her leggings. "I just wanted to wait until you got home so I could see you were safe."

Something stirred inside him. Something primal. No one had ever waited to see if he was okay. Nobody had ever gone to the trouble of checking up on him. Oh, Mac and Braden checked in, but they were friends, brothers.

Laney was…special.

"I didn't think you'd mind if I used your code."

She'd only been to his house once, but every O'Shea had his code for emergency purposes and he had theirs. This was clearly an emergency for her. That primal feeling turned into a warmth he didn't want to recognize.

"But now that I can see for myself you're okay, I'll just go." She was adorable when she was nervous. "I'm sure you're tired and need to rest."

Ryker moved closer as she rambled, his eyes never coming off that lip she was biting. She'd been scared—for him. More scared than he'd ever seen her—for him. She was the most beautiful sight, and after the hellish past day and a half, he needed something beautiful in his life. He needed Laney.

"After we left things, and then we couldn't get in touch with you—"

His mouth slid over hers, cutting off her words. His arms wrapped around her waist, jerking her flush against his body.

Finally.

He felt like he'd waited forever to have her in his home, in his arms again. There were countless reasons why he shouldn't have been doing this, why he should've let her walk out that door.

But he needed this. He needed her, and he hadn't realized how much until he'd walked in and seen her curled up on his couch.

Laney melted against him, her fingers threading through the hair at his nape. Her mouth opened to his instantly, and Ryker didn't hesitate to take everything he wanted from her.

He wanted to devour her, wanted to take her into his bedroom and lay her flat out on his bed, taking his time the way he should've in Miami.

Laney was in his home, and this was one fantasy he'd had for way too long. No way in hell was he turning her away. He needed this. They needed this.

Before common sense or those red flags could wave too high, Ryker secured his hold around her waist, never breaking away from her lush mouth. He lifted her up, arousal bursting through him when she wrapped her legs around his waist.

"I didn't think you wanted me," she murmured against his lips.

Ryker spun and headed toward his bedroom. The sleep he'd needed moments ago was no longer on his radar.

"I never said that. Ever."

Laney nipped at his lips. "You push me away."

Ryker stopped, pulled away and looked into those engaging eyes. "Do you feel me pushing you away now?"

Her hips tipped against his as her ankles locked behind his back. "I wouldn't let you at this point. But what about tomorrow? Next week? What then, Ryker?"

On a sigh, he closed his eyes and rested his forehead against hers. "Right now, Laney. Let's concentrate on right now."

She hesitated a second longer than he was comfortable

with, but finally nodded. "I'm going to want answers, Ryker. I'm going to want to talk, not fight, about us."

About us. Those words terrified him and thrilled him at the same time. He'd worry about that conversation later. Right now he had the only woman he'd ever wanted in his bed actually here. He sure as hell wasn't going to talk, not when his emotions were raw. He had Laney and that was enough.

The second he crossed the threshold to his master suite, he hit the panel on the wall to close the blinds, encasing his room in darkness—much like the way he lived his life. Laney was the brightest spot he'd ever had, and he didn't need anyone to tell him he didn't deserve her, or their baby.

But heaven help him, he wanted both.

Laney tucked her face into the crook of his neck, her warm breath tickling him as he led her to his bed in the middle of the room. Easing down, he laid her on his rumpled sheets. He hadn't made a bed in…well, ever.

As much as he wanted to follow her down, he pulled back because he had a driving need to see her splayed out. He'd never brought another woman into his house, into his bed. If he thought too hard about this moment, he may let fear consume him, but he latched on to his need for Laney and shoved all else aside.

Her long shirt pulled against her breasts, her hair fanned out on his navy sheets and her eyes held so much desire, he didn't know if he was going to be able to take his time.

"If you are reconsidering, I'm going to kill you myself."

Ryker couldn't help but laugh. He reached behind his back and jerked his T-shirt over his head, flinging it across the room. Her eyes raked over his chest, his abs, lower. Pure male pride surged through him. He kept in shape and had never cared what anyone thought of him, not even his lovers, but he wanted Laney to care. He wanted her to…hell, he didn't know. There was nothing of worth in him, yet she wanted him. He was humbled and proud at the same time.

Laney sat up on the bed, pulling her shirt over her head as she went. Ryker was rendered speechless at the sight of her in a pale pink bra that did little to contain her full breasts. And when she reached behind her to unfasten it, staring up at him with those wide eyes, Ryker's control snapped.

With a need he couldn't identify, Ryker reached down and gripped the top of her leggings and panties. In one jerk he had them off and flung over his shoulder.

Laney lay back on his bed, a smug grin on her face. Ryker couldn't get his jeans unfastened fast enough.

"You think you've got me where you want me?" he asked, remembering he still needed to get his damn boots off.

She lifted one bare shoulder. "I've got you where you want to be."

No truer words were ever spoken.

After freeing himself from everything, he placed a knee on the bed beside her hip. Laney trailed her fingertips up his bare leg, sending shivers through him. Damn shivers. He was trying to keep some semblance of control here, but one touch from her and he was powerless.

Ryker glanced to her flat belly, worry lacing through him. He glanced up to see her smiling.

"It's fine," she assured him. "I promise."

He was clueless when it came to pregnancies or babies. Hell, he couldn't even deal with his own emotions, let alone care for another person. What was he thinking? Why was he letting his desire for Laney cloud his judgment?

"Hey." She reached for him, her fingers wrapping around his biceps. "Don't. Wherever you just went, come back. We'll deal with it later."

The war he'd battled with himself for years had no place right now. He couldn't deny her, couldn't deny himself. She was right. Whatever they needed to deal with could wait.

Laney eased her legs apart, tugging on him until he settled right where he needed to be. With his hands on either side of her head, he lowered onto his forearms so his hands could be free. He smoothed her hair away from her face, letting his fingers linger on her smooth skin.

"My scarred hands don't belong on you," he whispered, the words spilling from him before he could stop himself.

"I don't want anybody else's hands on my body," she purred, arching into him. "You're perfect."

Perfect. A word never associated with him before, let alone said aloud. Laney closed her eyes, blowing out a slow, shuddering breath. Ryker slid his body against hers, finally taking the time to appreciate how incredibly they fit together.

Laney flattened her palms against his back, urging him even closer. Her knees came up on either side of his hips as she let out a soft sigh. He couldn't take his eyes off her as he watched her arousal consume her. She could easily become a drug that kept him addicted forever.

But forever wasn't in his vocabulary. Forever wasn't a word for a man with his lifestyle.

"Tell me if I hurt you," he muttered. "I mean, with the baby…damn. I just don't—"

She leaned up, capturing his lips. "We're both fine."

Ryker captured her hips once more and rolled them over so she was straddling him and he was on his back. She sat straight up, her hands resting on his abdomen.

"I like this view better." He could look at it forever.

Damn that word for creeping into the bedroom again and making him want things he had no business wanting.

"You're letting me have control?" she asked, quirking her brow.

Ryker reached between them, rubbing his fingertip against her most sensitive part. Laney gasped, throwing her head back.

"I'm still in control, baby. Always."

Laney shifted, and in seconds settled over him, joining them, and Ryker's eyes nearly rolled back in his head. She was a vixen and she damn well knew it.

Her hips shifted, slowly. Too slow. Agonizingly slow. Enough.

Ryker gripped her hips between his hands and held her in place as he slammed into her at a feverish pace.

Laney's fingers curled into his bare skin, her nails biting into him. Perfect. This was what he'd missed. Her passion, her need for him that stirred something so deep within his chest, he refused to analyze it.

Laney tossed her head, her hair flying to cover part of her face. She clenched her eyes shut as her knees tightened against his sides. Ryker held his palm over her stomach a second before curling his fingers back around her side.

Mine.

The word slammed into him as Laney cried out her

release, and there was no stopping his now. Ryker's entire body trembled as he let go, Laney's pants only urging him on. He locked his eyes on her, shocked to find something in hers. Something much more than desire, much more than passion.

Damn it. Laney had love in her eyes. Love for a bastard who didn't deserve her, who'd betrayed her brothers. Love for a man who'd been told he was unlovable for the first twelve years of his life.

Ryker shut his eyes. He couldn't face this now. Not when he'd told her they'd talk later, not when he was feeling too damn exposed, and not when he knew there was no forever for them.

Eight

Monday morning had Laney heading to O'Shea's, the actual office in downtown Boston. Apparently there were some computer issues Braden needed fixed ASAP, per an employee's plea. Braden had told her this was top priority in an early-morning text.

Laney had only met the newest employee a handful of times, but based on what she'd seen of her and how she'd corresponded with her via emails and texts, Viviana was exactly the type of professional, poised person the business needed. The woman had been with them for nearly a year now and was proving to be an extremely loyal, trustworthy team member. She fit right in with the O'Shea family.

Laney let herself into the old building, which had been renovated into something of grand beauty back in the fifties. A few modern touches had been added to keep the ambiance up-to-date, and for security purposes, but overall, the building had been restored to its original grandeur. The old etched windows were kept, as well as the intricate trim and crown moldings. Scarred hardwood floors had been buffed and refinished to a dark, sparkling shine.

They wanted potential clients to feel at home. Because that's what O'Shea's was all about. Family.

Shaking off the cold, Laney turned and smiled at Viviana. The striking beauty was around the same age as Laney's brothers, but she could easily still be carded. She had glossy black hair, almost as if she had some Native American heritage. Her dark eyes and skin only showcased how gorgeous she was naturally.

"I nearly froze just walking in from my car," Laney stated, tugging off her gloves.

"Maybe I'll ask for a transfer to Mac's store in Miami," Viviana joked, her painted red lips parting in a stunning smile. "Just during the winter months. Boston can be brutal."

Laney nodded in agreement, recalling the snowstorm nearly a year ago when Braden and Zara ended up trapped together. Of course, if not for that storm, Zara may not be in the family now.

Laney couldn't imagine being trapped with Ryker. Actually, if their encounter two days ago was any indicator, their private time would be absolutely glorious. Maybe being trapped together would do them some good. Then he couldn't run away from what they shared and he'd have to listen to reason.

But Laney knew if they were alone, their clothes would be off and that would be the end of talking.

"We love you too much here to let you go," Laney replied, heading toward the back office. "Braden said the new program was giving you fits?"

Laney glanced at the framed images lining the walls. Ancestors in front of the store, some of her grandfather and father at the auction podium, another of her great-grandfather at his desk in the backroom...the same desk she was heading toward.

Viviana fell into step beside her. "I tried to go back through some records to find a piece we auctioned last spring in London, but the program shows a blank, like nothing was entered until two months ago."

Two months ago Laney had installed a simpler program; she'd put all the history of their auctions on there for easy access. Something was definitely wrong.

"Let me take a look." Laney moved into the spacious office and circled the antique desk her great-grandfather had found at an estate sale in Spain. This piece was part of O'Shea's history, passed down through generations. "Do you have any clients coming in this morning?"

Viviana crossed her arms her plum suit jacket and shook her head. "Not today. I was hoping to get some pieces logged in to the system. We've already received quite a few framed pieces of artwork and several items from a recent estate sale Mac handled in Naples."

Laney settled into her comfort zone behind the screen. She pulled up the system she'd created and saw everything was up-to-date from the time she'd installed it. Then when she tried to retrieve backdated records, the files were completely empty. That was impossible. Everything should have been in chronological order just like she'd programmed.

"If you want to work, you can still get into the system

to add new items. You just can't go back." Laney didn't look up as she continued going from screen to screen to see what happened. All of her codes were still as they should be. "I'll let you know if I need you."

Laney's cell chimed from her purse, which was on the leather club chair beside the door. "Would you care to grab that for me?" she asked without looking up.

Scrolling down the screen, Laney dissected each and every entry she'd made. Nothing was off, but—

Wait. She scrolled back up. That couldn't be possible. She stared at the screen again.

"Something wrong?" Viviana asked.

Laney leaned closer to the computer, sure she was mistaken. But she didn't want to say anything to anyone until she could research things further. Braden would explode when he found out about the security breach. Still, she wanted to double-and triple-check everything before she went to him with this. There was no need to alarm anyone if she was misreading everything...but the odds of her being wrong were pretty much nil.

Her stomach turned. Who would hack into her system? Who had the balls big enough to go up against the O'Shea clan? How the hell had anyone gotten through all the security she'd installed?

The answer was simple. They weren't hacked. This was an inside job.

"Laney?"

Fury raged through her as she turned to look at Viviana, who held out Laney's phone. "You sure everything is okay?" she asked.

Laney nodded. "I think I've found the problem, but it's going to take some time to fix. I'm going to take this laptop with me. Can you use one of the others?"

Viviana's eyes widened for a second before she glanced around the office. "Of course. Is there anything I can do?"

Be on the lookout for the enemy?

"No. I've got it handled." Laney looked at her phone, still in Viviana's hand. "Oh, thanks."

She saw Ryker's name on the screen and opened the text. She'd left him sleeping the other night because she knew if she'd actually stayed, she'd want to spend every night there.

She had to make Ryker realize he wanted this. Perhaps if she wasn't so available, he'd ache for her the way she did for him. She wanted him so needy for her, so desperate to have her in his life, he'd ignore his demons and take a chance. She wasn't playing a game, she was simply opening his eyes to what they had.

Pulling up his message, she read:

We need to talk. Meet at Braden's now.

Laney closed the program and shut the laptop. "I need to go. Call me if you have any more issues, no matter how minor."

Viviana nodded and scooted back, and Laney headed toward the office door. "Of course."

Laney tossed her phone back into her bag. Pulling on her wrap coat, she knotted the ties before grabbing the laptop and sliding it into the side of her bag, as well.

"There haven't been any strange calls or emails, even from regular clients?" Laney asked as she slid the bag onto her forearm.

Viviana shifted, her head tipped as she glanced at the floor. "I can't recall any. It's pretty black and white here," she told Laney, looking back up. "You think someone has been messing with the system?"

"I think it's a possibility, and I want you to keep your eyes and ears open. Call me, not Braden or Mac, if you notice anything odd."

She'd figure out what was going on in the meantime.

"Of course," Viviana stated.

Laney headed through the main part of their office area and back out into the swirling snow. The streetlights lining each side of the street were decorated with simple, elegant evergreen wreaths with bright, cheery red bows. The garlands twisting around the poles ran from the wreath to the base. The city was battling the snowfall by keeping the sidewalks salted, the streets cleared. Laney absolutely loved her hometown of Beacon Hill and never wanted to be anywhere else.

As she climbed behind the wheel of her car, she wondered what Ryker wanted. Did he actually love Boston like she did, or did he love the lifestyle he led of traveling, going from one adventure to the next? Would he slow down, take fewer risks now that he was going to be a father?

Knowing Ryker...no. He would think he could do it all, as if he were invincible.

She headed toward her childhood home and pulled in behind Ryker's SUV. Large, menacing, just like the man himself. That whole dark, mysterious persona he oozed was so damn sexy, but there was infinitely more to Ryker. The layers that made up that man were tightly woven together, but she wasn't giving up on removing each one until she uncovered the very heart of him.

Grabbing her bag from the passenger seat, she got out of the car, careful where she stepped this time. Watching the ground before her gray boots, she started when a pair of black boots came into view.

"Easy." Ryker gripped her arms to steady her. "I came to make sure you didn't fall again."

Laney's heart flipped. She didn't want to keep sliding further in love with him, but there was no way to stop. Regardless of the baby, Laney loved Ryker. She'd love him even if they'd never kissed or slept together. Nothing could ever diminish her feelings for him.

"Well, startling me is not the way to go about helping."

Ryker took the bag from her arm and slid his other arm around her waist. "I wouldn't let you fall. Ever."

"If you keep tossing gallant gestures my way, I'm going to think you're trying to get all romantic."

Those dark eyes locked onto hers. "I don't do romance, Laney. I do reality."

Laney rolled her eyes. The reality was that she loved him, and he could ignore it all he wanted, but he had feelings for her, too. She wasn't offended by his words, not when his actions were booming louder than ever. Laney was optimistic that Ryker would come around... the question was how long would she give him before she finally told him how she truly felt? If she pulled out the cringe-worthy *L* word at this point, he'd sprint back into his steel shell and never come out again.

Ryker was vulnerable, not something she'd ever say to him or he'd ever admit, but the truth was glaring them both in the face. The don't-give-a-damn attitude, the rough exterior he offered to the world, wasn't who she saw. She looked beneath all of that and found the man he truly was...a kind, gentle and generous man with so much to give, one capable of so much love. It was a man he probably wasn't even aware existed. Or one he was battling to keep inside.

Regardless, Laney was about to rip his mask off and shove him in front of a mirror.

"Ankle okay today?" he asked.

"Just tender, but nothing I can't put weight on."

His arm didn't leave her waist, which was fine with her. She wanted his hands on her, and clearly he wanted them to be there.

"We have a problem."

Laney froze on the sidewalk, jerking her gaze up to his. "What?"

After the security breach, she didn't need more bad news. Dread curled in her stomach.

"We had a call from one of our contacts with the Bureau." Ryker ushered her toward the steps. "Let's get you inside. It's too cold out here."

"No." Laney placed a gloved hand on his chest. "First tell me what he wanted."

Ryker clenched his jaw. "Apparently someone is feeding them information. Intel only someone in our organization would know. They've discovered some pieces of art that are in our computer system, that only we have the log for. And I know you put those in like any other items we obtain legally, but they have a list of our back auctions."

Laney pulled in a breath, the air so cold her lungs burned. "This isn't a coincidence," she murmured.

Ryker's grip on her tightened. "What?"

"I have something on my laptop to show you guys. Let's get inside."

She could pull up any company document on a family computer, but she was most comfortable working with her own. She knew what documents and files to access right from the start. Time was of the essence.

As she turned, everything seemed to shift all at once. She tilted, thankfully against a firm, hard chest.

"Easy," Ryker told her, his arm around her waist tightening. "What happened?"

Laney held a hand to her head, shutting her eyes. "Just got a bit dizzy, that's all."

Before Laney could say another word, her world tilted again as she was swept up into Ryker's arms. "Put me down. I can walk."

"And I can carry you and your bag, so be quiet."

There it was. That emotion he held so hidden within him, one he didn't seem to recognize. If she thought for a second he didn't want her, she'd let it go. But when she saw a need in him, a need that matched her own, she couldn't ignore the facts…or let the best thing in her life slip right by because she was afraid to take a chance.

Laney wrapped her arms around his neck, nestling her face against the heat of his. She closed her eyes, relishing this pivotal moment. The baby would not be a tool in this path she was on to show Ryker how much she loved him, and that's not what this moment was about. Right now, he cared about her.He wasn't about to let her fall or get hurt. Laney only prayed by the time this was all said and done, that would still be the case.

She also refused to let him fall. She'd do anything to keep the man she loved safe. She was an O'Shea. The fact she was a female made no difference because she was brought up to be strong, fierce and resilient. Nothing could stop her from staking her claim.

"What happened?" Braden's worried tone brought her out of her thoughts. "Did she fall again?"

Ryker brushed by Braden and into the warmth of the house. "No. She started getting dizzy."

Ryker eased her down because it wasn't as if he could hold her forever. Shame that. Plus, if she clung to him too long, Braden would get the idea something was going on. Which reminded her that they were going to have to tell her brothers soon. Their unknown reactions terrified her.

"I'm fine," she assured them both, offering a smile. "See? Standing on my own two feet."

"Did you eat breakfast?" Braden asked, his brows still drawn together in worry. "Go sit in the living room, and I'll bring you something."

"No, no." She waved a hand, then opened the ties on her coat. "I ate. I must've just moved too fast, and with all that's going on with work, I'm just stressed."

Oops. Wrong choice of words. Ryker's eyes darkened, narrowed. His lips thinned.

"You'll be taking it easy. I'll make sure of it."

He delivered the threat in that low, sexy tone of his that left no room for argument. Laney merely nodded because now she was facing down two of the most alpha men she knew.

"Have a seat anyway," Braden told her, gesturing toward the living room.

Laney headed into the room that screamed Christmas: from the sparkly garland draped over the mantel, to the twelve-foot-tall noble fir standing proudly in front of the old windows, to the various candle stands, berries and other festive decor.

Quite the opposite of Ryker's house. Not one sprig of evergreen was to be seen there. A testament to what he came from. The child who didn't do Christmas had turned into a man who didn't, and it was one of the saddest things Laney had ever seen.

She took a seat on the high wing-back chair her mother had fallen in love with at an estate sale when she and Laney's father had first gotten married. Patrick O'Shea had never been able to say no to his wife. Their love, though cut too short in Laney's opinion, was something Laney wanted. That love, the family, the bond was what Laney dreamed of. And they weren't little girl dreams. She was going into this situation with Ryker knowing full well she could get hurt, but the chance of a love and family of her own was worth the risk.

Weren't O'Sheas built on all the risks they'd taken? A challenge was never avoided, but met head-on. And conquered.

"Ryker told me you had a call from the Bureau," she started, not wanting to waste any time. "I don't know what all you found out, but Viviana's problem at the office was the system's backlog. I was looking into that when I got Ryker's text."

Ryker leaned one broad shoulder against the mantel, crossing his arms over his chest. "Tell me what you found."

Braden remained standing as well, right by the leather sofa across from her. The tension in the room was palpable.

"When I go into the records, there is nothing showing from before I changed systems," she explained. "Everything should be in the files I added by year and then broke down into months. Before October, there is nothing."

"Define nothing," Braden said between gritted teeth.

Laney faced him, staring into eyes exactly like her

own, exactly like their father's. "Not one document is on there. Don't worry, I have backups of everything at home. I'm not sloppy, Braden."

"I never said you were, but what the hell is going on and what does this have to do with my call from the Feds?"

"When I first started digging to see what happened, it appeared someone hacked into our system. But that would be virtually impossible."

There was no easy way to deliver such a statement, so she went for it.

"The only way someone could access the system is if they work for us. My security is so tight—"

"Not tight enough," Braden growled.

Laney straightened her back, squared her shoulders.

"Chill, Braden." Ryker's warning couldn't be ignored. "Respect."

Braden turned his attention across the room. "She's my sister, I can damn well say what I want."

"No, you can't." Ryker's sneer even made Laney shiver. "She's the best programmer I've ever met, and I know some shady bastards."

Even though she could've handled herself, and her brother was justifiably angry, Ryker's quick defense warmed her. He'd always protected her, but he'd never spoken back to Braden in such a manner.

"Who the hell are you to tell me?" Braden countered. "We may be facing a real issue here, not to mention the scrolls are who knows where. But the Feds are on our back and our system was hacked? Doesn't take a genius to figure out we have a mole."

The idea horrified Laney. They were so careful about who they hired. The background checks were extensive, their training and "babysitting" period was just as meticulous. Now the question was how did they narrow their search down to one office? They had branches all over the globe. Their main one, of course, was in Boston, and a year ago one opened in Miami and in Atlanta.

Could the traitor be one of the employees down South?

"We need to warn Mac," she stated, thinking aloud. "He needs to start scouring his crew while we look at ours. We clearly should start with our US locations. I doubt the threat is coming from overseas. That wouldn't make any sense."

Braden nodded. "I agree. What I want to know is how someone fractured your system."

Laney rubbed her forehead, wondering the same thing. Closing her eyes, she willed the slight dizziness to pass. Maybe she should get some orange juice or something in her stomach.

"I'm going to figure that out." Laney eased back in the chair, rested her elbow on the arm and opened her eyes. "I took one of the laptops from the office, and I plan on looking through its history. I'll do the same for the rest of them."

Braden's hardened gaze held hers. "I love you, Laney. I'm not doubting you. I'm shocked, actually. We've never had this kind of breach before, and the last thing I need is the Feds sniffing around."

Since Braden had taken over after their father's passing, the O'Sheas had been moving into more legitimate territory—which meant staying off the radar of the law. To her full knowledge, they'd been so careful. Minus Ryker and Shane's incident, there wasn't anything that she knew of that would cause this level of scrutiny...well, she still didn't know what happened to her ex.

What a mess. Having the Feds involved did not bode well for the O'Sheas.

"I promise you, there won't be a problem. I'll get this fixed, and we'll find out who the snitch is."

She risked a glance at Ryker, who looked even more menacing than usual. Those dark lashes fanned out over coal-like eyes, his hard-set jaw was clenched, his arms were crossed over that impossibly broad chest. Ryker was pissed, and she only prayed she could get to the bottom of this betrayal before he took matters into his own hands.

Nine

Laney had just grabbed a bottle of water when her front door slammed. Because she lived in an old brownstone, she didn't have that whole open-concept thing going on. She liked her rooms cozy and blocked off into designated areas.

"Hello?" she called as she made her way to the front of her house.

She wasn't too concerned about an intruder, considering she had alarms, cameras and an insane security system she knew her brother and Ryker had paid quite a bit for. They'd insisted on making sure she was safe the second she moved out of the O'Shea mansion.

The bottle crinkled in her hand as she stopped in the entryway to her living room.

"What are you doing here?"

Without taking his eyes off her, Ryker jerked out of

his leather jacket and tossed it onto the couch. "I'm making sure you're okay, and then I'm helping you get to the bottom of this damn mess."

Nerves stirred in her stomach. He was here because he cared, and he was here for work. Their worlds collided on so many levels, there was no way she could find separation.

"I'm fine."

"You were dizzy earlier, then you weren't feeling well when you were talking with Braden."

Laney twisted the cap on her bottle of water and took a drink. He hadn't made a move to come in any farther, but clearly he was staying since he'd taken off his coat. This was becoming a habit...one she would gladly build on.

"I was feeling a little light-headed while we were talking. It passed."

"You're not driving anymore."

Laney screwed the lid back on and cocked her head, sure she'd heard wrong. "Excuse me?"

Now he moved, like a panther to its prey. He crossed to her until they stood toe to toe, causing her to tip her head back to meet his intense, heavy-lidded gaze.

"You heard me."

"I did," she agreed. "I'm giving you the chance to choose different words."

A hint of a smile danced around those kissable lips. "I'm not backing down on this, Laney. Until your dizzy spells pass, I'll be your chauffeur."

Even though she knew he wouldn't back down, Laney waited a minute to see if he wanted to add anything...or retract such a ridiculous statement.

Finally, when he said nothing, Laney stepped around him and headed toward the corner of the sectional she'd been cozied up in. Well, as cozy as one could be while working on discovering who hacked into her family's computer system. Clearly the O'Sheas were smarter than to have all of their skeletons exposed for anyone to see. But there were items, especially in the past when her father was at the helm, that could be looked at twice. Some may find their "mysterious" auction pieces to be a red flag, considering the majority of them had been reported stolen.

Laney eased back into the curve of the couch and picked up the laptop she'd laid to the side.

"Glaring at me and using this whole silent predator vibe definitely will not change my mind," she told him without looking at him. She typed in the password for the laptop. "So, did you want anything else? Or are you ready to move on to work?"

Laney had just pulled up the system, but before she could go any further, a delicate pewter ornament appeared between her and the screen. Jerking her eyes up to his, she gasped.

"What is that?" She looked back to the ornament. "I mean, I know what it is, but—"

Well, damn. There she went, tearing up. She hated all these pregnancy-induced crying jags.

She reached out to take the likeness of a woman wrapping her arms around her swollen belly. The simple pewter ornament would look absolutely perfect on her white-and-silver tree. She clutched it against her chest.

But when she looked back up, Ryker glanced away, shoving his hands in his pockets. "I wasn't sure what to get. I mean, I didn't set out to get anything, but I was passing by that Christmas shop near the office."

"All Seasons."

He nodded. "Yeah. I knew you liked that place since you mention it every year."

Her favorite little shop because they literally transformed their store into a completely different place depending on the season. She could spend a fortune in there...and she had. A fact he well knew because he'd taken her there a few times when he felt she was in danger of being in public alone. Of course he'd kept his brooding self out front or waiting in the car at the curb.

"They have a tree in the window that reminded me of yours, and it caught my eye," he went on. He looked at his feet, the wall, the tree...anywhere but at her. "Then I saw this and..."

How adorable was he, being all nervous? This was definitely a side of Ryker Barrett she'd never seen before. Laney set the laptop aside and came to her feet. Tears flooded her eyes as she held tight to this precious gift.

She slid her arms around his neck, tucking her face against his. "This might be the sweetest thing anyone has ever got me."

Slowly he returned her embrace, and Laney wanted to sink into him. "You deserve more," he whispered into her ear.

She knew he wasn't talking monetary items. Ryker could buy her an island and a private jet to get there if he wanted. There was a fear in Ryker that allowed him to touch her, yet not get too emotionally involved. He felt he didn't deserve her, but she was just getting started in proving him wrong. He was everything she deserved.

"This doesn't mean you're driving me," she muttered.

Ryker laughed. The vibrating sensation bounced off her chest. "We'll talk about that later."

There wasn't going to be a later for that particular

topic, but he'd find out soon enough. They didn't have time to argue.

Laney pulled back, kissed him briefly, then shifted from his hold. Crossing the room to the tree, she hung her ornament right in the center, then stepped back to look at how perfectly it fit.

"I love it," she said, turning. "You didn't have to get me a gift, but it's my new favorite decoration."

Ryker nodded, which was about as much of a reaction as she was going to get from him.

"Now, we need to get to work because whoever is fighting us has chosen the wrong family to mess with."

Before she could settle back onto the couch, Ryker's arm snaked out and wrapped around her waist, pulling her against his hard chest. He closed the space between them, covering her mouth with his. Heat, instant and all-consuming, swept over her as she wrapped her arms around his neck.

All too willingly, she opened to him. He eased her back slightly, keeping his hold on her tight, protective. Laney threaded her fingers through his hair, wishing they didn't have to work, wishing they could go to her bedroom and use this kiss as a stepping-stone to something much more erotic and satisfying.

When he pulled back, nipping at her lips, Laney waited for him to say something…anything.

"I'm not complaining," she started when he remained silent. "But what's going on between us? You keep me in your bed the other day, you buy me the sweetest gift ever and now you kiss me like your next breath depended on it."

Ryker's hands slid to her hips where he held her still. "I have no idea," he stated on a sigh. "I can't put a label on this. I only know I did want you in my bed all day, I knew you had to have that ornament and just now my next breath did depend on kissing you."

Laney stared into his dark eyes, eyes that had terrified many enemies. Eyes she'd fallen in love with when she'd been only a teen. She'd seen him come and go many times while she'd been in high school. While her friends were out at the malls or movies with other boys, Laney was home waiting on Ryker to show for a meeting with her father. She'd get a glimpse of him as he'd come into the house. When she was lucky, he'd turn his gaze toward her, meet her with that intense stare for a half second before moving on to the study.

That split second had been worth skipping a night out with her friends.

"Don't fight whatever is happening," she told him. "And don't be afraid of it."

Ryker grunted. "I'm not afraid of anything, Laney. I think you know that."

Again, she wasn't going to argue. They didn't have the time. But he was so terrified of his feelings, he refused to even acknowledge them. Or perhaps he didn't even know they existed.

She eased back into her seat, set her water bottle on the cushion next to her and pulled the laptop back into her lap. Ryker grabbed the large ottoman from the accent chair and pushed it in front of her.

"Put your feet up."

Laney waited a second, but he merely raised a brow and continued to glare. Okay, no point in arguing. Propping her feet up, she started pecking at the keys. Ryker stood.

"It's going to be a while, maybe even days. Might as well have a seat."

"We don't have days."

Laney prayed she would find something that would lead them in the right direction. "You think I don't know that, Ryker?" She didn't even bother to spare him a glance as she worked. Time was of the essence—the only reason she didn't pursue that kiss. "I'm an O'Shea, a glaring fact my brothers and you often forget. I know what's at stake."

Laney ignored the silence as she scrolled through code after code. Let Ryker process her words because it was rather ridiculous how they attempted to keep her sheltered at all times, but expected her to twinkle her nose at the first sign of a computer problem. She wasn't naive; she knew exactly what her family did, what they stood for. She also knew Braden was doing his best to make sure they kept their reputation impeccable within the auction world while cleaning up their act on the legal side. Well, as much as it could be cleaned up. She knew Ryker had done things at her father's request...

She shut her eyes, forcing away any mental images. A shudder rippled through her.

"Laney?"

Instantly he was at her side. Sure. Now he chose to take a seat.

"I'm fine," she assured him. "Just a chill."

More like a clench to her heart. That was the part of her family's past she preferred to keep under wraps. She knew there were justifiable reasons for their actions, she even knew there were times it was self-defense. She'd been fifteen years old when she'd overheard a twenty-five-year-old Ryker describing a trip to Sydney to her father. Ryker had been telling Patrick about a guard who'd attacked him with a knife. Laney recalled standing on the landing of the house, curled up on the floor and holding on to the banisters in the dark. At that moment, she'd realized how dangerous Ryker's job truly was and what he put on the line for her family.

"I don't know how the hell you comprehend all that," Ryker muttered.

Laney kept scrolling, slowly, looking for any hint as to how their security had been breached. She knew the threat was on the inside. Which meant if she had to access every employee's computer, she damn well would.

Her mind kept returning to the timing. The newest stores had been opened a year ago in Miami and Atlanta. The Boston office had been around since the beginning. Where was the mole more likely to be?

Laney didn't know how long she searched. Losing track of time was an occupational hazard. Her stomach growled, and she waited for Ryker to make some snarky comment, but when he remained silent, she glanced over. The man was out. Head tipped back on the cushion, face totally relaxed. Laney wasn't sure she'd ever seen him this peaceful, this calm.

When Ryker was in work mode, which was nearly every time she saw him, he was hard, intense, focused. When they were intimate, well…he was exactly the same way.

Laney's hands went lax on the keyboard as she studied his facial features. His brows weren't drawn in, his mouth was parted just slightly, as if waiting for a lover's kiss, black lashes fanned over his cheeks. She could study him forever.

Forever. If she even said that word to him he'd build yet another wall to protect himself.

Without tearing her eyes away from him, Laney slid the computer off her lap and onto the cushion beside her. She tipped her head back on the cushion as well, needing just another minute of this. One more minute of nothing but Laney and Ryker. There was no outside world, there was no issue with work and there was no fear of telling her brothers that she was expecting Ryker's baby.

Given how fiercely he protected her, Laney knew he would be an amazing father. He doubted himself, but she'd be right there showing him how perfect he was. She wasn't experienced at being a mother, but she knew love. Between her love and his protection, their child would have everything.

Laney bit her lip to keep from tumbling into that emotional roller coaster that seemed to accompany pregnancy. She shifted her thoughts to what their baby would look like. Dark hair for sure since they both had black hair. But would the eyes be green or coal-like? Would Ryker's strong jawline get passed down?

Suddenly those coal-black eyes were fixed on hers. "How long are you going to stare at me?"

Ten

"You scared me to death," she scolded him, swatting his arm. He lifted his lids and couldn't help but smile.

Ryker had known the second Laney had stopped working. He'd heard her stomach growl and was about to say something, when he'd felt her shift. The sudden awareness of her eyes on him had him holding still. He'd felt the slightest dip in the cushion next to his head, and he wondered what she'd been thinking.

Then he'd worried where her thoughts were. He knew Laney had dreams of a big family. She had that innocence about her that would cling to romance and love. She had hope. He'd lost that when he'd been in diapers.

"Find anything?"

Laney kept resting her head on the cushion next to his. "Nothing new. We've already established that it was an inside job. Braden doesn't like hearing that one of his employees is a mole, but we have to find out who it is before they cause more damage."

Rage burned in his gut. There wouldn't be a hole deep enough for this bastard to hide.

"Don't." Laney's hand slid up his forearm. "I'm furious, too, but don't let it ruin this moment. I just want a minute more of no threats, just us."

Us.

"We're always threatened." Unable to resist, Ryker flipped his hand over and shifted to lace their fingers together. "The authorities who aren't on our side are always looking for things to pin on us. On me."

Laney closed her eyes. Ryker hated this. Hated wanting her with an ache that was indescribable. Hated that he couldn't have her fully because of who he was. Hated most of all that he was the one who put worry into that beautiful life of hers.

"I can't stand the thought of you being hurt, being a target." She met his gaze once again. The fear in those eyes gutted him. "I've known for years how much you put at stake, but now it's different."

"The baby—"

"And me." She leaned forward, resting her forehead against his. "Before the baby, before Miami. I started falling for you."

He'd known. Hell, he'd known for years, but hearing her say the words seemed so official and real. He couldn't have her committing herself to him. There was no future for them as a couple, only as parents to this innocent child. That's all they could share.

But, damn it, he couldn't hurt her. He couldn't reject this gift she'd just presented. Laney was everything perfect and pure in his life. She was that place in his mind he went to when he was on assignment and the world around him turned ugly. She'd been his salvation for so long...but telling her that would only give her false hope.

"I know you don't want to hear those words." She eased back, leaving Ryker feeling cold. "But I can't lie to you."

He didn't know what to say, so like a complete moron, he said nothing. Laney shoved her hair away from her face and turned to get her laptop, instantly diving back into her work. The moment was gone.

Ryker reached over, gripping her hand beneath his. Her fingers stilled on the keys. She kept her eyes on the screen, her throat bobbed as she swallowed. Nerves were getting to her, he needed to at least reassure her...what? What the hell could he say? Ryker had no idea, all he knew was he wanted that helpless look gone.

"I'm out of my element here, Laney." He decided to go with honesty. "You've been part of my life for so long, but—"

"I know," she whispered.

How could she know when he didn't know himself?

"No, you don't." Damn it, he needed to make her understand. "You can't possibly know what I feel. You have no clue what those words mean to me."

Her head dropped as she pulled in a deep breath. "I know you better than you think," she said quietly.

Silence settled heavily around them. Ryker had never been this close to a woman. He'd had lovers, mostly when he traveled and needed a stress reliever. The possibility of a serious relationship had never entered his mind. It had no place in his life.

"I know who you are," she went on, still not looking his way. "I've known all along."

Now she did turn, those vibrant green eyes piercing him right to his soul. Until now he hadn't even been aware he had one.

"I know full well why you're trying to keep me at a distance. I'm not backing down, Ryker. You need to know that I intend to fight for what I want, and I want you."

Laney's words should have terrified him. But damn if her fire wasn't the sexiest thing he'd ever seen.

"I'll consider myself warned."

Her eyes narrowed. "If we weren't in so deep with this traitor mess, I'd show you right now how much I love you. That will have to wait."

Ryker's body stirred. He'd never put his work second to anything or anyone before…but right at this moment he was seriously considering doing just that.

"Get that look out of your eyes." She laughed. "How about I keep working and you go see what you can find in the kitchen?"

Ryker came to his feet. "Because I'm all for equal rights, I'll cook for you. But I expect you to open doors for me and buy me flowers."

Laney laughed, the exact response he was hoping for. He couldn't handle tension…not with her.

"That wasn't sexist at all," she said, grabbing a throw pillow and smacking him.

That smile lighting up her face never failed to warm him in spots only she could touch. Guilt slammed through him. There was no way in hell Braden and Mac were going to allow their baby sister to have a relationship with Ryker, even if he thought he could risk it. No, Laney's brothers were looking out for her, and they would be justified by telling her *hell no* when it came to Ryker.

Baby or not, the O'Shea brothers wouldn't budge in

this area. They'd had him follow Laney's boyfriends over the years. Ryker had investigated worthless jerks, and he'd scared off the ones who posed any threat to Laney or the O'Sheas in general. Each time he'd had to intervene, Ryker had selfishly felt relieved that Laney wasn't going to be with some jerk any longer.

Now here he was taking that role...and Mac and Braden were going to have to be the ones to talk some sense into Laney because he sure as hell had no willpower where she was concerned.

And she was wrong. This baby did change everything. Ryker knew he'd never be the same again.

Dinner consisted of chips, salsa and, surprisingly, a taco salad. Apparently Ryker's favorite food was Mexican, and he'd made it happen. She hadn't known those ingredients were in her kitchen, but Ryker had worked a miracle and produced something amazing.

Hours later, Laney's eyes were crossing. She closed the laptop and glanced across to Ryker, who was on his phone, leaning against her newly decorated mantel.

"I'm waving the white flag," she told him around a yawn.

He straightened, shoving his cell in his pocket. "It's nearly one in the morning. You need to sleep."

"What about you? You need sleep, too."

Looking at him in her living room, all dark and menacing, he actually seemed to fit. Amid the sparkling tree, the garland, the Nutcrackers and especially the new ornament, Ryker worked perfectly in her living room, in her life. He'd been a sport and had hung the rest of her ornaments and even added the newly fluffed wreath to her front door. He did draw the line sprinkling the iridescent glitter across the silver and white decor on her mantel..

But he'd stayed. He'd brought her living room to life with Christmas, made dinner and put the empty storage boxes back in her attic. There was something to be said about a man who put his woman's needs first. And she was his woman. He'd figure that out on his own soon enough.

Ready to make good on that promise to fight for what she wanted, Laney set the laptop to the side and came to her feet.

"You need sleep, too," she repeated, slowly closing the space between them. "It would be ridiculous to go out in this weather."

His half-lidded perusal of her body from head to toe and back up sent shivers racing over her, through her. The man's stare was nearly as potent as his touch. She practically felt him when he licked his lips as if she were a buffet. And he could devour her anytime he wanted.

"I'm not afraid of snow," he told her.

Taking a risk that the hunger in his eyes was his weakness, Laney gripped the hem of her shirt and pulled it over her head, tossing the garment to the side. His eyes remained fixed on her, exactly where she wanted them.

"But why take the chance?" she asked, reaching around to unhook her bra.

In a flash, Ryker reached out, wrapping those strong hands around her upper arms. For a second she feared he was going to stop her. Then she focused on his face. Clenched jaw, thin lips, desire staring back at her.

"You want me to stay?" he growled. "Then I'll be the one doing this."

He tore away her bra, jerked down her pants and panties. She had to hold on to those broad shoulders as he yanked the material over her feet. Standing bare before him sent another thrill through her. He stood back up, his hands roaming up the sides of her body, over the dip in her waist, cupping her breasts. His thumbs brushed against their peaks.

Laney couldn't help but lean into his touch. But then his hands moved back down. His hands covered her stomach.

"No matter what happens with us, this is all that matters. I'll do everything to protect our baby."

Laney nodded. There was so much uncertainty between them, but the baby's security was top priority. Until the arrival of their child, Laney would show him just how much she loved him, how much he deserved to be loved.

"If that means you have to move to my house in London, then you'll do it." She started to say something, but his hard eyes stopped her. "I'm serious, Laney. We don't know what we're dealing with, and I'll be damned if I take a chance with our baby."

Fear fueled his words. She knew this unknown threat had him as worried as the rest of them. Now was not the time to bang her chest and be all independent. They were a team.

"I promise," she whispered as she went up onto her toes to slide her lips over his. "Anything you want."

Ryker's hands shifted to her backside. Pulling her flush against his fully clothed body, he growled. "I want to take you up those stairs and keep you locked in your bedroom naked for the next week."

Oh, if only…

"But all I can promise is right now."

He kept saying that. All of these "right now" moments were adding up. Did he notice? He would. One day he'd wake up to the fact they were it for each other. Laney dared her brothers to even try to stop her happiness.

"Then show me," she muttered a split second before his mouth came crashing down onto hers.

He lifted her with ease, carrying her toward the staircase as his lips demanded everything from her…and promised so much more. As if she weighed nothing at all, he took the four steps onto the landing. Just when she expected to feel him turn and head the rest of the way up, he stopped. Laney tore her mouth away, ready to ask him what he was doing, but she found herself being eased onto the built-in, cushioned bench.

She tipped her head back to peer up at him, the soft light from the lamp in the living room casting a perfect yellow rim around his frame. She had no idea what he intended to do, but he reached behind his neck and jerked his T-shirt over his head. After he tossed it behind him, he quickly rid himself of his black boots, sending them back down the steps with a heavy thunk.

Laney couldn't take her eyes off that impressive chest. Spattered with dark hair, a scar over his left pec and a tattoo of a menacing dragon over his right, Ryker was all man…and he was still stripping.

"This is the best show I've ever been to."

The snap to his jeans popped open, he drew the zipper down, all without taking his eyes from hers. "I don't want to hear about the time you and your friends went to Poppycocks."

Laney gasped. "You know about that?"

"Baby, I know everything about you, and I sure as hell am not getting into this now, nor are we discussing the fact I had to do damage control with your father and tell him you were at the mall."

Laney bit her lip to keep from laughing because Ryker clearly didn't find the humor in her sneaking into a male strip club when she was only seventeen. Those fake IDs she'd made for herself and her friends as a joke had come in handy.

Laney opted to keep her mouth shut and enjoy the view as Ryker ridded himself of the rest of his clothes. Unable to keep her hands still, she reached out. She needed to touch him, explore him. Every time they were together her ache for him grew.

Ryker took her hands before she could touch him. Jerking her to her feet, he tugged her until she fell against him.

"I'm calling the shots here. No touching."

Laney quirked a brow. "Then this night is a total bust if I can't put my hands on you."

Strong arms banded around her waist, and instantly she was lifted once again. Laney wrapped her legs around him as he continued up to the second story.

"I'll tell you when you can touch me," he ordered. "I'm going to lay you down and do this right. We're always in a hurry."

Laney rested her head against his shoulder. "Does this mean you're staying all night?"

He reached the double doors to her bedroom and shouldered them open. Looking down into her eyes, Ryker nodded. "I'm staying. Saying no to you is becoming impossible. I don't know what the hell that means, but for now, I'm staying."

Laney knew exactly what that meant. It meant Ryker was hers, and he was finally, *finally* coming around.

Eleven

Ryker rolled over in bed. The canopy with white sheers draped all around the posts was definitely not his bed. This was Laney's world, a world she'd graciously let him into.

No. Scratch that. A world she'd woven him into, and he was getting to the point where he wasn't sure if he ever wanted to leave. It would be the smart thing to do, but he had needs, damn it…and he wasn't just talking physical.

He had no clue what time it was, but the sun wasn't up yet. The soft glow from Laney's phone had him squinting to see what she was looking at.

Baby furniture. Something twisted in his gut. All this time he'd been worried about their safety, about how he'd handle Mac and Braden. The reality was this child would need things. Probably lots of things he had no damn clue about. But he'd learn. He refused to be a deadbeat dad like his had been. Ryker would go out of his way to make sure his child, and the mother of his child, was comfortable and wanted for nothing.

Ryker slid an arm around Laney's waist, flattening his palm on her stomach. "I'll buy whatever you want," he murmured, nuzzling the side of her neck.

The warmth of her body penetrated him, never failing to warm areas that had been iced over for years.

"I can get the things for the nursery." She scrolled through a variety of white cribs. "I really want yellow and white, no matter the sex. I can always add accent pieces once we find out what we're having."

Ryker swallowed. This was a conversation he never, ever thought he'd be having…especially with his best friends', his *employers'*, little sister.

"Do you care what we have?" Laney turned her head slightly to look at him.

Ryker eased back. "I hadn't thought about it, actually."

Blowing out a soft breath, she turned back toward her phone. "No, I'd say you haven't. This isn't something that excites most men, and when you weren't wanting a baby at all—"

Ryker lifted enough to roll her beneath him until she was on her back and staring up at him. He rested his hands on either side of her head.

"A baby may not have been on my radar before now, but that doesn't mean even for a second that I'm not excited about this life, Laney."

Her face lit up. Her brows rose, a smile spread on her lips. "You're excited?"

Hell. He hadn't realized he was excited until he'd said the words aloud.

"I am. I'm scared as hell, though. I haven't thought

about the sex because it doesn't matter to me." Ryker kissed her softly. "All that matters is you two are safe, healthy, happy. That's my goal here, Laney."

Cupping the side of his face, she stared back at him. Her brows were drawn in, the happiness in her face vanished.

"I'm scared for you," she murmured. "When Braden and Mac—"

He silenced her with his lips. "I'm not worried about them."

"They won't like this." She blinked as moisture gathered in her eyes. "They'll blame you, and I've been half in love with you my whole life, and Miami was—"

"Amazing." He nipped at her lips, her chin, along her jawline. "Miami had been coming for a long time. There was no way I could've avoided you forever."

The screen on her phone went dim, plunging the room into darkness. He settled perfectly between her spread thighs.

"I can resist many things in this world, but you're not one of them." He ran his lips along the side of her neck as she arched her body against his. "I'm only human, Laney. And I can only ignore my body for so long. I've told you before, I'm a selfish bastard."

"No, you're not. You're one of the most giving people I know." Her arms and legs encircled him as he slid into her. "You know this is more than just the baby and chemistry between us, right?" she asked.

Ryker stilled for a second before moving his hips slowly. "I can admit that, yes. But beyond that, let's just—"

"I know. Concentrate on now." She returned his thrust

with a quicker pace. "I'm all for what's happening right now."

But they would get back to this topic later, he knew.

Ryker framed her face between his hands again and covered her mouth with his. He'd never wanted to take his time like this, never wanted to enjoy the process of getting to the climax. Fast and frantic had been just fine with him. Slow, passionate…that meant getting more emotionally involved.

And God help him, he had plunged headfirst into this…whatever this was…with Laney.

Her nails bit into his back. She opened her mouth fully for him, completely taking him in every way she could. There was a fire, a burning for her that hadn't been there before. The all-consuming need he'd had in the past was nothing compared to right here, right now. She was taking him and wrapping him into her perfect world where she believed such things as love actually existed.

Ryker tore his mouth from hers, ran his lips down her neck, to one perfect breast. Her hands came up to his head, as if to hold him in place. Her soft gasps only fueled him further to make sure she had everything she wanted.

"Ryker…"

He eased back, then pushed forward hard. Once, twice. Her entire body shuddered beneath his. It was almost too much to bear as Laney cried out his name, arched beneath him and came undone all around him.

And it was all Ryker needed to follow her over the edge.

The papers for the new property had been signed a few days ago, the contractor had been hired and Laney couldn't wait to get her hands dirty and dig into the process of renovating the old, neglected building in Southie.

Right now, though, she was having a difficult time breathing in the damn dress she'd purchased for O'Shea's annual Christmas party. She'd thought it was fine in the store, but, the overflowing cleavage and the slight pull of the emerald green satin at her waist gave her pause. She hadn't noticed her midsection getting any larger, she was only eight weeks pregnant now, but something had happened overnight because she was seriously worried about popping that side zipper.

"Being so gorgeous and built like that should make me hate you."

Laney spun to see Jenna, her arm looped through Mac's. Crossing the ballroom, Laney threw her arms out wide.

"I'm so glad you guys made it in." She hugged her brother before turning to Jenna, taking in the gorgeous red dress that highlighted her curves. "Like you're one to talk. You look stunning."

Jenna had a voluptuous figure, not model-thin like some women felt they needed to be. Jenna was a beautiful woman and looked even more striking now that she was in love. Mac, Laney's globe-trotting playboy brother, had finally been tamed by his best friend when he had to pose as her fiancé. Laney would've given anything to see the moment her brother realized Jenna was the one. She had seen this coming for years and couldn't be happier for the two of them.

"I was worried the snow would delay you all getting here."

Mac shrugged. "I checked the area before I took off."

Her brother doubled as a pilot. "I was confident we'd be safe. If not, we could've gone into DC and rented a car."

"He'll fly in almost anything," Jenna joked. "He's had me white-knuckling it more than once, but he assures me he has everything under control."

Mac's pilot's license came in handy since he hated Boston winters and was now living it up in Miami.

"Next year I vote we move this party to my house," he suggested. "Too damn cold up here."

"Are you complaining already?" Braden stepped into the room, Zara by his side. He slapped Mac's shoulder. "You haven't been in town an hour and already a hater."

Laney noticed Zara scanning the room and tuned out her brothers' banter. "I came a little early and made sure all the centerpieces were set up like we'd discussed. I hope you like them."

Her sister-in-law smiled. "They're beautiful."

"You're beautiful," Laney countered. "That gold dress is perfect on you."

"I think we all look amazing." Zara continued to look around, her brows drawn in a frown. "Is Ryker here? I thought he told Braden he'd be here early."

Laney's heart quickened. It had been several days since he spent the night in her bed. He'd gone out of town on business to acquire some authentic pieces for the spring auction. He'd only gone to Toronto, then to Chicago, but she hated not knowing he was in town. Not that she ever felt at risk, but she definitely felt safer knowing he was around.

"He's in the study," Braden stated. "He…had to take a call."

A call? Why had Braden hesitated? Laney knew Ryker's personal life was technically none of her business, but she still wanted to know what was going on. And if Braden had been in the study with Ryker, then the call was most likely business…in which case she still wanted to know.

"The room looks amazing," Jenna said as she pulled away from Mac's side and started walking around. "The lights, the tables, all of it looks magical. You all really know how to treat your employees."

"Loyalty deserves to be rewarded," Mac stated simply. "And O'Shea's wouldn't throw a cheap party."

"Neither would I," Zara chimed in. "I totally use you all to boost my own company."

Braden smiled, leaned down to kiss his wife on the head. "You do an incredible job. You don't need us."

Her brothers had found two amazing women to share their lives with. Laney wanted to tell them all about the pregnancy, but she wasn't ready. Beyond the fact that she worried how they'd treat Ryker, Laney wanted to tell Zara privately so she didn't have to absorb the news around others. Zara would most likely be elated, but Laney didn't want to take any chances. The miscarriage was still fresh, but did that loss and ache ever really go away?

Laney prayed she never had to find out.

She pulled in a breath, as much as her dress would allow. "I'll be right back."

She wasn't going to make up an excuse to leave the room. The guests weren't due to arrive for another hour, so her presence wasn't needed at the moment.

The foursome continued talking as the caterers entered through the side doors to set up the food tables in the back of the room. Laney saw her chance to slip out. She headed toward the wide, curved staircase and made her way up to the study. Nobody would think twice about her and Ryker talking.

Once she reached the landing, she glanced over her shoulder to see that she was still alone. She didn't hear Ryker on the phone as she approached the study, then she realized the door was closed. Laney turned the knob slowly as she pushed the door open a crack. When she peeked inside, she didn't see Ryker on the phone at all. His hands were on the desk, his back to the door, his head bowed.

Opening the door wider, Laney let herself in. Her heels were quiet on the carpet, but the shift in the full skirt of her dress pulled Ryker straight up. He spun and froze. Laney stilled, as well.

She'd seen him in a tux before, but something about seeing him now that she knew him so intimately…damn, he was one sexy man. His all-black tux played up the menacing male he was on a daily basis, but the expensive cut screamed money and class. Ryker was every type of fantasy man wrapped into one delicious package.

And something was troubling him. His tight face, clenched jaw and worried eyes stared back at her.

"What's wrong?"

Shaking his head, he pushed off the desk and walked toward her. "Nothing now that you showed up wearing this killer dress."

As much as her ego appreciated his approval, she wasn't letting his compliments distract her from digging deeper.

"Tell me." She stepped back when he stood right before her. Touching him now would get them nowhere… except naked, which was a bad idea, considering her family was downstairs. "Something happened."

Raking a hand over the back of his neck, Ryker blew out a sigh. "Nothing for you to worry about."

When he reached for her, Laney held up her hands. "No. You're not blowing me off. I do worry, Ryker. It's what happens when you care about someone."

"It's just work, nothing I can't handle." He moved lightning-fast and wrapped his arms around her, pulling her body flush with his. "You didn't tell me you'd look so damn sexy tonight. I'm going to have a hard time keeping my hands to myself."

Laney wanted his hands all over her, but she also wanted to know what he was hiding from her.

"You better keep your hands off. If we expose ourselves here, you and my brothers will have a fight and that's not the atmosphere we want for this party."

"I'll just have mental foreplay until I can get you back to my bed tonight."

Laney lifted a brow. "Your bed?"

He slid one fingertip up her arm, across her collarbone and down to the V of her plunging neckline. "My bed. Where you belong."

Laney could barely process the meaning of those words for all the delicious tingles shooting through her. Finally, he was coming around and admitting he wanted her. They were making progress and she was going to continue to build on this, to show him exactly what they could be together.

Ryker's eyes held hers, so much desire and passion staring back at her. She couldn't get to his house soon enough.

The click of the door had Ryker easing his hand away and crossing his arms over his chest. Laney took a step back.

"Everything okay?"

Laney kept her back to Mac, who'd just come in. Her eyes stayed on Ryker, who was looking over her head.

"Yeah. Laney was just following up on an email she sent me earlier."

When Ryker moved around her, Laney turned in time to see the one-armed man hug between the two.

"I hear we got the Feds on us now." Mac shoved his hands in his pockets and rocked back on his heels. "If you all need me here, let me know. I doubt the source is coming from down South."

Laney shook her head. "I disagree. I think the timing is too coincidental, since you opened two new stores and now we have a mole."

"We can't rule out anything yet," Ryker, the voice of calm and reason, interjected. "I'll pursue every angle, and Laney will dig deeper to get to the bottom of this. She's been losing sleep over it."

Mac's eyes darted to her. "You can't take on all of this by yourself."

Guilt hit her hard. "I set up the system, I did background checks on every employee. By default, the blame comes back to me."

"We don't work that way," Ryker told her, his gaze hard. "We're a team. Remember?"

The burn in her throat, the prickling sensation in her eyes came out of nowhere. Now was not the time to cry. But damn him for reminding her of that fact.

"He's right," Mac agreed, oblivious. "We're all in this together, and we'll get out of it together. We just have to pool our efforts like we always do."

Laney pulled in a shaky breath and nodded. "You're right. I still feel responsible, but I will get to the bottom of this. I just need more time with the computers to eliminate our main office as the source of the snitch."

"Not tonight," Ryker told her. "Tonight we're all taking a few hours off and not worrying about work. We have enough Feds in our pocket to hold them off for a bit."

Between the Feds and worrying about the baby and when to drop that bombshell, and trying to analyze Ryker's sudden change of heart about sleeping with her, Laney had a headache. No surprise there.

She rubbed her forehead and closed her eyes for a moment. The guys continued to talk, and she willed the oncoming migraine to cease. Maybe it would help if she ate something. The caterer they'd hired was the best in the area. Laney's mouth watered at the thought of the filet mignon on the menu, and the chocolate fountain and fresh fruit sounded amazing, too.

"Laney?"

Ryker's worried tone had her opening her eyes, offering a smile. But the smile was moot when she started to sway.

Instantly Ryker took one of her arms and Mac had the other.

"You all right?" Mac asked.

Laney nodded. "Just getting a headache. No big deal."

She glanced between her brother's worried expression and Ryker's questioning gaze. She knew where Ryker's mind was, but she couldn't reveal too much here.

"I'm fine, I swear. I just need to eat, that's all."

Ryker's grip on her elbow tightened. "Then let's go downstairs and get you something."

Nodding, Laney pulled from both strong holds. "I can take care of myself. I'll just go into the kitchen and grab some crackers to hold me over."

"No, you'll eat more because when guests arrive, you'll be talking, and you'll forget to get a plate for yourself."

Laney stared at Ryker and he glared right back. While the whole protective thing was cute and sexy, she couldn't stay around him during this party. Their guests—her family—would be on to them in a second. Laney saw how Zara and Jenna stared at their men, and Laney knew for a fact she had that same love-swept gleam in her eye.

"I'll grab some fruit or something, too," she assured him. "I'm fine."

Without waiting for another argument, she turned from the guys and headed out of the room. Once in the hallway, Laney leaned against the wall, held a hand to her stomach and took a moment to relax. She needed to stay focused on finding who was betraying her family, but she couldn't neglect her body. This baby was everything to her. She'd wanted a family of her own since she could remember, and she'd been given this gift. It might not be how she had pictured things would fall in line, but did life ever really work that way?

Laney pushed off the wall and headed downstairs. She needed to get a hold of herself and put on her game face. This night had to be about the company and her family. And discovering the traitor in their midst.

Twelve

Ryker moved about the room, never straying too far from Laney. That damn dress was going to be the death of him. He wasn't sure if he wanted her to leave it on later when they were alone or if he wanted to peel it off of her. Those curves, the breasts that threatened to spill out and the fact she was carrying his baby were a lethal combination.

"You think our betrayer is here?"

Ryker gripped his glass of bourbon and nodded to Braden. "Yeah, I do. I think the bastard wants to keep close, thinking if they didn't show up, we'd see it as a red flag. They'll act like the doting, perfect employee."

"Damn it." Braden took a sip of whatever he was drinking, *Scotch by the smell of it*, Ryker thought, and let out a sigh. "I knew they'd be here. When I find out who I opened up my home to, my family to, they will be sorry they ever crossed us."

Ryker scanned the room. Laughter, chatter, hugs, everything seemed like a regular O'Shea's Christmas party. Women wore glamorous gowns and the men wore their finest suits. The tradition had been started decades ago. Before the O'Shea clan had taken him in, he never would've dreamed this was where he'd end up. A boy from a broken home with a deadbeat, druggie father had turned into a billionaire by simply being loyal and valuing what family was all about.

And Ryker would do it again even without all the money.

Zara joined them, swirling her glass of wine. "I'd say this party is another success."

Braden nodded. "Of course it is. I married the best event coordinator in the world."

Ryker listened, but his eyes were on Laney. She was chatting with Viviana and whoever her date was. Some guy with a beard and an expensive suit. Ryker had never seen the man before, but he'd met Viviana and knew the family trusted her. Laney hugged the woman and turned, her gaze catching Ryker's. His heart kicked up as she made her way across the floor. The way her body shifted, the way that dress hugged her until mid-thigh then flared out, those creamy shoulders exposed…he was going to have to think of something else because Laney was seriously killing him. And from the smirk on her face, she damn well knew it.

"Feeling better?" Braden asked when Laney stood before them. "Mac said you'd gotten dizzy or something earlier."

"I'm fine."

"You're not taking care of yourself," Braden added.

"This is the second time this has happened recently. Have you been to the doctor?"

Laney nodded. "I have, and I promise I'm perfectly healthy."

Ryker hated this. Hated lying to the only people he truly cared about.

"Have you tried this white wine?" Zara asked Laney. "It's the best I've ever had. I already asked the caterer the name, and I'm going to order it for my next event."

Laney shook her head. "Wow, it must be good."

"Let me get you a glass," Zara stated.

Ryker froze at the same time Laney's eyes widened. "Um, no. I'm just going to have some water for now."

Zara's brows drew in. "Are you sure?"

"Positive."

Ryker needed to move this conversation in a different direction. Laney was uncomfortable, and that was the last thing she needed.

"Braden, are you—"

"Oh, Laney." Zara's words cut him off. "Are you... are you pregnant?"

The last word was whispered, and Ryker gritted his teeth. He scrambled for a defense, but he couldn't outright lie. It wasn't as if they could keep the baby a secret forever. Damn it, he wanted, needed to come to Laney's aid here, he just had no idea how.

"Laney?" Braden jerked his attention to his sister. "Are you?"

The party went on around them, but the silence surrounded their little group, blocking everything else out. Ryker opened his mouth, not sure what he was about to say, but Laney's one word response cut him off.

"Yes."

"Oh, honey." Zara stepped forward and hugged Laney. "I'm sorry. I just blurted that out because I recognized the symptoms. I shouldn't have said anything."

Laney returned the embrace. "It's okay. I was waiting to tell you all. I wasn't sure how you'd take the news."

Zara leaned back. "I'm happy for you if you're happy. Braden and I are confident we'll have children, so don't worry about me."

Laney's smile widened as she turned her attention to Braden. "Well, do you have something you want to say?"

"Who's the father?"

His low, anger-filled tone cut right through Ryker. To Laney's credit, she didn't even flick a glance his way as she continued to smile.

"Right now we're just keeping things low-key. I'm not ready to say who the father is just yet."

Part of Ryker was proud of her response, honest but still keeping their secret. The other part of him, the bigger part of him, hated the fact he was kept out of the equation. He wanted to be part of this child's life from the start. Not hidden in the background.

And he sure as hell didn't want Laney defending him. That wasn't how this was going to work. He may not know where the hell they were headed, but he wasn't going to hide behind a pregnant woman.

"I'm the father."

He ignored Laney's gasp and concentrated on Braden…who slowly turned his eyes to Ryker.

"You're lying," he stated in a low, threatening tone. "You'd never do that to me."

Laney reached forward, putting her hand on Braden's arm. "Don't. Not here."

Braden shrugged her off. "I will kill you myself."

Ryker clenched his fists. "You can try."

"No bloodshed." Laney stepped between them, her back to Ryker. "Now is not the time to discuss this."

Zara tugged on Braden's arm. "She's right. You need to step back, and we can all talk after the party."

Braden's hard eyes never wavered from Ryker's. This was his brother and he'd betrayed him. Ryker didn't blame Braden for wanting to kill him. Whatever Braden, and Mac, threw his way, Ryker knew he deserved every bit of it. But the worst part, the scariest part, was the possibility that he'd no longer be part of the family.

Braden shifted his attention to Laney. "What the hell were you thinking?"

"My personal life is none of your business," she spat.

"What is going on?" Mac moved to the group, Jenna right on his heels. "You all are causing a scene."

"Laney's pregnant and Ryker is the father." Braden delivered the blow to Mac in a disgusted tone, but never took his eyes from his sister. "She was just about to explain what the hell she was thinking."

"I wasn't about to explain anything to anyone," Laney said, lowering her voice. "I don't owe any of you a defense. And I sure as hell am not getting into this here."

When she turned away, Braden reached out and snagged her arm. Ryker saw red.

"Get your hand off her," he gritted out. "Or I won't care what type of scene we cause."

Braden's anger was palpable. Ryker would gladly take the brunt of his rage, but he refused to have Laney shoulder the blame.

"This isn't the place," Mac stated. Ryker glanced to him, but was met with equally angry eyes. "But we are going to talk when this party is over."

Ryker nodded in agreement. Laney jerked free of Braden's grip and gracefully walked away. She wasn't going to cause any more of a scene than necessary, and he applauded her for her poise and determination. Ryker, on the other hand, was ready to throw his fist through a wall.

"Come on, Braden. You have a party to host." Zara wrapped her arm through his. "Getting angry isn't going to change a thing."

Braden remained still for several moments before being led away. Ryker turned to Mac and Jenna.

"You want to say something now?"

Mac's jaw clenched. "Later. I'll have plenty to say later."

"What your sister and I do is none of your concern."

Mac's sneer indicated otherwise. "You got my sister pregnant. I'd say every bit of this is our business, *brother.*"

The parting shot did the damage Mac had intended. He walked away, leaving Ryker feeling even more like a bastard than he already did. He'd never thought he was good enough for Laney—and her brothers had just hit that point home.

There was no certainty how things were going to go down, but Ryker vowed to keep Laney safe. He'd told her he wouldn't let her get hurt, and he damn well meant it.

Oh, he wasn't concerned her brothers would physically harm her. No way in hell would they do that. But words could cause more damage than any actions, and tensions were running high.

Ryker felt for the souvenir penny inside his pocket, the reminder he needed right now. Family was everything to him, and he'd slashed right through that shroud of trust.

Now he had to pick up the pieces and make some vain attempt to put them all back together.

Laney's nerves were shot. She didn't have the energy to argue with her brothers, and she was furious at Ryker for dropping their bombshell the way he had. She'd had things covered, she was trying to keep him out of the hot seat until her brothers had a chance to process the pregnancy.

And she could think of so many other times that would've been more appropriate.

The caterers were gone, the room now a skeleton of a beautiful Christmas party. The employees had all mingled, chatting about the upcoming spring auction, the biggest one of the year. Laney had tried to zero in on who she thought could be capable of betrayal, but after the intense scene with her brothers and Ryker, she had lost focus.

"I'm so, so sorry, Laney."

Laney turned toward the doorway to the ballroom leading off the foyer. Zara had her hands clasped in front of her as she worried her bottom lip.

"None of this is your fault." Laney moved toward her sister-in-law and let out a sigh. "I have no idea where the guys went, but I hope Ryker is still alive."

Zara nodded. "Braden and Mac are outside, and I saw Ryker go up to the study. Jenna is finishing up in the kitchen, but I wanted to slip out and see you without the others."

Tears pricked Laney's eyes. "I was so worried how you'd take the news. I didn't want to bring back all of those memories."

Zara reached out, taking Laney's hands in hers. "The

memories are always there. The hurt will never go away, I imagine. We are trying to have another, and my doctor says he sees no reason why we can't get pregnant again. Don't worry about me, Laney. This is a special time for you and Ryker."

Laney blinked back the burn and moisture. "I don't know what Braden and Mac are going to do. I mean, they're all like brothers, they're best friends. Ryker needs them in his life. He had no one before coming here. He—"

"You love him," Zara said softly.

There was no denying the truth. "Yes."

"Then fight for this. Your brothers are in a state of shock, and most of their anger stems from getting caught off guard. Make them see how much you care for Ryker. Does he feel the same way?"

And wasn't that the question? How did Ryker feel? The man was so closed off. She knew full well how he felt about their physical relationship, and she was almost positive he had feelings for her, but she wanted him to say it. To admit how he felt and stop hiding from everything.

"It's okay." Zara squeezed Laney's hands. "Go on upstairs. Your brothers will be up shortly, I'm sure."

Laney wrapped her arms around Zara. "I'm so glad you're in our lives."

Returning the embrace, Zara whispered, "Me, too."

Pulling herself together, Laney made her way upstairs. She wasn't ready for this talk, didn't think she'd ever be. She knew going in that harsh words were going to be exchanged, some things that could never be taken back. But she wouldn't let her brothers blame Ryker. That was an issue she refused to back down on.

When she eased open the study door, she saw Ryker

across the room, facing the floor-to-ceiling windows be-hind the desk. With his hands in his pockets, he looked as if he didn't have a care in the world. Laney knew dif-ferent. He carried everything on his shoulders.

She closed the door at her back, and the click had Ryker glancing over his shoulder.

"You need to leave," he told her, turning back to look out the window. "I've got this."

Yeah, carrying the entire weight, as if this pregnancy was one-sided.

"We're a team, remember?"

She moved across the floor, nerves swirling in her stomach. If he shut her out now, Laney didn't know how she'd handle his silence.

"Why didn't you let me manage things earlier?" she asked as she came to stand beside him. When he didn't look at her, Laney's heart sank just a bit more.

"I don't want you to think I was keeping your name from them for any reason other than it wasn't the time or place to get into this."

Ryker whirled, eyes blazing with fury. "I'm not hid-ing behind a woman. You think I was just going to stand there and let Braden speculate? How would that have worked out for either of us when he did find out the truth? If we'd let that go, his rage would've been worse."

Once again, Ryker was the voice of reason. Plus, it wasn't his style to let a woman take the fall, especially her. She should've known he wouldn't stand by while she made excuses and skirted around the truth.

"I just want to go home with you and be done here," she whispered.

"I'm not sure that's the best idea right now."

Laney froze. "What? Don't even tell me you're letting them come between us already."

He turned back to stare out at the dark night, illuminated only by the glow from the patio lights below. "I've told you before there is no 'us.' Their reaction should have told you that."

Laney crossed her arms over her chest. "And we're not going to fight them on this?"

The muscles in his jaw clenched. His silence might as well have been shouted through a bullhorn.

The door to the study opened, then slammed. Laney glanced up to see her brothers. Furious over Ryker's stance, Laney had had more than enough.

"If you're going to come in here and beat your chests over how you're supposed to protect me and Ryker knew better, save it." Laney glared across the room as her brothers started in her direction. "I'm expecting a baby. We didn't plan it, but your anger won't change a thing."

Mac stopped behind the leather couch and rested his hands over the back. "Maybe not, but we're still pissed. We're family, Laney. Ryker crossed the line."

Laney rolled her eyes. "I assure you, he didn't make the baby himself."

"So what now?" Braden asked, his eyes on Ryker. "What do you plan to do with my sister?"

Laney stilled, her back turned to Ryker as she waited on his response.

"I plan on helping her raise our baby and continuing to keep her safe. This changes nothing."

Laney's heart broke. Cracked right in two, then splintered into shards on the ground. She wasn't going to beg anymore. She'd tried to show him how perfect they'd be together, but clearly he wanted to keep that bit of distance in place so he could hold together the only family he'd ever known. She understood his fear, admired him for clinging to what he'd built, but to throw away her love was the last straw.

Laney turned to face Ryker. "You're right. This changes nothing. We're going to have a baby, but that's all."

Those dark eyes stared back at her. Lips thinned, jaw clenched, he was seething. Laney continued to stare, tipping up her chin in defiance. If he wanted to expand, then he needed to do so now. If he wanted to come to her "rescue" like he always had in the past, he needed to say what he felt. Why did have to be so set on doing the right thing? He was human, and they were attracted to each other. He'd showed her with his actions that he cared. Why was he choosing her brothers over her—again?

"We have too many problems going on right now for you two to be at odds," Mac cut into her thoughts. "Laney, are you feeling okay? Are you sure you can keep working?"

Throwing her arms in the air, she spun. "For heaven's sake, I'm pregnant, not terminal. I've had a few dizzy spells, but that's all normal."

Braden ran a hand over the back of his neck and glanced toward the ceiling. Laney waited for the back-lash.

"Don't take this out on Ryker—"

"Stop, Laney."

She glanced over her shoulder. Ryker had turned from the window. His dark eyes held her in place, and she wanted to say so much more. She wanted to beat some sense into him until he relaxed his moral compass. He was so damn worried about getting shut out, he was lit-erally letting her slip away.

"I'll handle my end," he told her.

His end? So they were on separate sides?

"Yeah, I guess you can." She swallowed the hurt, ignoring the threat of tears. She had no time for tears, she was too angry. "I'm going home. I'm tired, I've had a long day."

Gathering the skirt of her gown in one hand, she marched toward the door.

"Laney."

Ryker's voice stopped her.

"I'll drive you home."

Letting out a humorless laugh, Laney turned. "Like hell you will. I can handle this myself."

Throwing his words right back at him should've made her feel marginally better, but she only felt empty. She shot a glance to each of her brothers.

"If I come across any new leads on the mole, I'll let you know."

She couldn't be in this room another second, and at this point she didn't care what they did to one another. They were all morons. Laney wondered how the hell she'd been cursed to be surrounded by idiots. Not one of them was thinking beyond this moment. Her brothers weren't looking to the future, to a new generation of O'Sheas, and Ryker was being so damn stubborn, she was getting another headache thinking about it.

By the time she got home, all Laney wanted to do was soak in a bubble bath and think about her precious baby. Designing a nursery in her head was exactly what she needed to relax. No work, no men, just sweet little baby thoughts.

Thirteen

Ryker's eye throbbed. He'd deserved the single punch to the face…hell, he had expected so much more. Braden had delivered the blow, and Ryker hadn't even attempted a block.

How could he fault them for being protective of Laney? Ryker had done several interventions on her behalf when she'd been with men who weren't appropriate. He expected nothing less from Braden and Mac.

But Ryker had hurt her. He'd lied when he said the baby changed nothing. This baby changed everything. He'd been void of emotion for so long, something uncomfortable kept shifting in his chest, and he was scared as hell. Not that he'd ever admit such a thing aloud. He'd meant what he said when he'd told her there was no "us." Even so, he couldn't seem to stay away.

Though it was late, Ryker found himself standing outside Laney's house. It was time for damage control. He didn't text her first, nor was he about to knock. He knew O'Sheas hurt deeply and wanted to be left alone.

Too damn bad.

Ryker let himself in, punched in her security code and locked the dead bolt behind him. The Christmas tree lit up in the corner drew his attention to the pewter ornament hanging front and center. She'd genuinely been surprised and happy when he'd given that to her. He'd never seen her smile like that, at least not directed his way. He wanted to see that again. He needed to know he hadn't damaged something inside her.

Damn it. He raked a hand through his hair. He knew more than most how deeply harsh words sliced, and once they were out, there was no way to take them back.

"What do you want?"

Ryker glanced up the staircase. Laney stood on the landing, belting her robe, her damp hair lying across one shoulder.

He remained where he was, though everything inside him demanded he rush up the stairs, grab her and beg for forgiveness. Pride wouldn't let him...the same damn pride that was making her hurt.

Why did he have to be such a bastard? Why didn't he have normal feelings like everyone else? He'd been fine with his callous ways...until Laney.

"I came to apologize, though I doubt you'll accept it."

Crossing her arms over her chest, she nodded. "You're right. Which brother hit you?"

"Braden."

"Neanderthals," she muttered before starting down the steps. "I should get you some ice."

Ryker paused. "You're going to play nurse after what happened?"

Laney reached the landing, her hand braced on the newel post. "Braden had no right to hit you because we slept together. That's none of his business. But don't mistake the bag of ice as my forgiveness."

Even when she was pissed, Laney wanted to help. She managed to do things to him, things he never thought possible. She made him feel as if he actually had a heart. Problem was, he had no idea what the hell to do with it.

When she reached the bottom step, Ryker pivoted just enough to block her. With her up just those few inches, she was at eye level and right where he wanted her to be.

"Don't make this more difficult," she whispered, biting her bottom lip. "I'm tired, Ryker. You said enough earlier."

Jasmine. She'd used some form of Jasmine soap or shampoo, or whatever other potion women used. And she smelled absolutely delicious.

"I didn't mean those words the way they came out," he told her, clenching his fists. He wanted to reach for her, was desperate to touch her, but he didn't want his other eye blackened. He may be desperate, but he wasn't stupid.

"Yet you waited until we were alone to tell me that." She quirked a brow. "Your apology is accepted, but the damage is done. Do you want ice or not?"

"No."

"Fine. Then let yourself out and reset the alarm. I'm going to bed."

Before she could turn, Ryker placed his hand over hers on the post. "I'm lost, Laney. I have no idea what the hell I'm doing."

Her hand relaxed beneath his, giving him a minor

hope she wasn't ready to shut him out. If there was ever a time to spill his thoughts, it was now.

"I can't lose any of you," he went on. "Do you understand that? You're all I have. Braden and Mac are my brothers. I have no idea where this is leading between you and me, but I have to have some stability. I know you think I'm some superhuman, unfeeling bastard right now, but I feel...too much."

Laney's eyes closed, and Ryker had no idea what she was thinking. Everything was new to him. He'd been infatuated with her for so long, but never thought anything would come of it. Yet, here they were, expecting a baby and trying to wade through this mess he'd made.

And she loved him. Words he could never, ever forget.

"I can't do this with you." Her misty eyes landed on his, touching him right to his soul. "You know how I feel and when you do this push-pull. I have no idea how to react. I get that this family is yours, I completely understand you can't lose us. But are you willing to ignore everything between you and me?"

The hurt in her tone destroyed him. Ryker couldn't stand another second, he had to offer some comfort, but he knew the comfort was mostly for himself.

Taking her face between his hands, he stared directly into those vibrant green eyes. How could she pierce him so deeply? Nobody had ever even come close to touching him the way Laney had. But if he risked everything, *everything*, and they fell apart, it would kill him.

He eased forward, resting his forehead against hers and pulling in a deep breath. "I need time."

"I've given you most of my life," she whispered. The direct punch hit its mark.

"I'm new here, Laney. I can't mess this up, for you, for our baby. Just…don't give up on me."

Silence settled heavily around them, and Ryker hated the vulnerability he was showing. But this was Laney, and he was starting to see exactly what it would take to keep her waiting until he figured out his jumbled emotions.

She didn't say anything, didn't touch him in return. Ryker knew he wasn't done baring his soul. Stepping away from her, because he couldn't slice himself wide open *and* touch her, he started pacing her living room.

"I had the sad, clichéd childhood," he began, ignoring that instant burn to his chest when he thought about those first twelve years. "My father was a user, a man-whore, a worthless piece of trash who never should've been allowed to keep a child. I witnessed more by the time I was five years old than most people see or hear in a lifetime."

Ryker stopped in front of the mantel, catching Laney's gaze in the large mirror hanging above the greenery. "He'd leave me alone for days. I stole food to eat, I got myself ready for school, I picked fights on the playground so I could go to the principal's office."

Bracing his hands on the mantel, Ryker lowered his head. "I just wanted any contact with a male adult. I didn't care if it was negative. They'd try to call my dad, but of course he never answered. Half the time our phone bill wasn't paid anyway. So I'd stay in the office and finish my schoolwork, which was what I wanted. I wanted to be left alone to do my thing."

Pushing off the mantel, he started pacing again. He'd never let his backstory spill out like that. But now that he'd started, he wasn't about to stop. Laney deserved this part of him, she deserved it all, but this is all he could give for now.

"When I saw your brothers in a fight, I was all too eager to jump in. My dad had been gone for nearly a week, and I was pissed. I needed to take my aggression out on someone."

"How did nobody notice this for twelve years?" Laney's quiet question broke through his thoughts.

"People are so wrapped up in their own lives." He shrugged and reached for the ornament he'd given her. He rubbed his thumb over the roundness of the silhouette's belly before letting it go to sway against the branches. "I was so skeptical about meeting Patrick, but the second I saw him, I knew he was one of the good guys."

Laney let out a soft laugh. "Only a select few would lump him into that category, but I agree. He was the best."

"From the second I came to stay with you guys, then started working with your brothers, I felt like I had a place, a real home. Braden and Mac treated me like family. You were so young at first, I ignored you. But once you got to be a teenager, I was looking at you in ways that I shouldn't. Had your dad had even the slightest idea of what my thoughts were, he would've killed me himself."

"You never looked at me twice," she stated.

Ryker threw a glance over his shoulder, just in time to see one of her cats dart up the steps and disappear. "I looked. I fantasized. My penance for lusting after you was to watch you grow into a beautiful woman, to see other bastards on your arm. Then when we saw how eerily good you were with computers, I realized my penance had just begun."

He moved to the wide window in the front of the

house. Staring out onto the darkened night, with only a street lamp lighting a portion of the view, Ryker was forced to look at his own reflection. Fitting, considering he barely recognized the man who was spouting off his life story.

Slipping his hand into a pocket, he pulled out the penny. "I have been just fine keeping my distance from you. I mean, I wanted you, but I knew you were on another level, and nothing between us could ever happen. I've never forgotten where I came from, no matter how much money I have in my account or how many houses I own."

When he turned, he found her exactly as she'd been moments ago. Standing on that bottom step, her hand on the post, her eyes never wavering from him.

Holding up the pathetic piece of metal, Ryker walked forward. "I keep this ridiculous reminder in my pocket of what I came from. I've had this with me every single day since I was ten years old."

He stood only a few feet away, but held the penny out for her. Laney took it, examined it.

"This is one of those flattened pennies with your name on it." She brought her eyes back to his. "What's this from?"

"My dad was actually sober for a few hours one time." How sad was it that Ryker could pinpoint the exact hours his dad had gone without a drink or a fix? "There was a carnival outside the city, and he took me. He got this with my name on it, maybe because he felt he owed me something. I have no clue why, but this was the only thing he'd ever bought for me. This was the only time in my childhood he'd actually taken me anywhere."

Laney's eyes filled as she clutched the penny in her hand. "Are you worried about being a father?"

"Hell, yes, I am." Ryker rubbed the back of his neck, glancing to the floor before going on. "What do I have to fall back on? What part of my past says I'm ready to help raise another human being? I won't leave either of you, but I'm scared as hell, Laney."

"You're not afraid," she countered, her voice softening. "You're refusing to accept what already is. You have all of these wonderful emotions inside you. I know you care for me, I know you care for this baby. If you'd let yourself relax, you'd see there's so much more than fear. Fear is a lie. If my father showed you nothing else, he showed you that."

"There can't be animosity between your brothers and me, or them and you. There can't be. This family needs to be unified, and I swore to your father we'd find those scrolls, we'd keep this family going. I promised, Laney."

Still clutching the penny, she crossed her arms and nodded. "And we'll continue to do just that. My brothers aren't part of what you and I have going on. You need to understand that because if you don't, then we have nothing."

"If I were Braden, I would've killed someone like me."

Laney's hard stare held him in place. Damn, when she got that look, she was every bit Patrick O'Shea's daughter. She meant business—and she was sexy as hell.

"Braden's not going to harm you. Well, other than the black eye."

"You're aware of the man I am, what I've done to keep your family safe."

Laney nodded. "I'm not naive."

"You never ask me, you never look at me as if you disapprove."

Laney shrugged. "I know my father had his reasons.

I know Braden wants no more violence and that you had to take care of Shane because he tried to hurt me." She swallowed, bit her lip and pushed on. "And I know when my ex disappeared—"

"I didn't kill him. I couldn't. I sent him away with a fat check and a promise that if he returned, he would be finished."

"I thought you…"

Ryker nodded. "I know what you thought. I let you think that because I was trying to keep some wall between us, but it didn't work."

Laney blinked, glanced around the room as if trying to process what he'd just said. "I'm glad you didn't hurt him, but why didn't you? You hated him."

Hate was such a mild term for the man who'd verbally abused Laney. The guy was lucky he was still drawing breath in his lungs.

"I didn't want you to look at me like I was a monster."

"I could never look at you that way."

Ryker took a step forward. "I couldn't take the chance."

Laney uncrossed her arms, handed the penny back to him and pulled in a breath. Ryker shoved the memento back into his pocket.

"How much did Braden give you to send Shane away?"

"He didn't give me the money."

Her perfectly arched brows drew in as she tipped her head. "You used your money?"

"I'd have paid him every last dime I had to leave. I didn't want to have his blood on my hands, and I wanted him out of your life."

Laney pushed her hair over her shoulder and clutched

the V of her robe. She'd looked so damn gorgeous earlier in that red ball gown. She'd nearly stopped his heart and was the envy of every woman there; she was also most likely most guys' fantasy tonight.

But right now, she stood before him, void of all makeup, wearing nothing but her silk robe and smelling like everything he didn't deserve.

"Don't shut me out," he murmured. "I need time, and I know it's not fair to ask, but...just don't push me away, even when I'm being a selfish bastard."

It seemed as if an eternity passed as he waited for her to say something. Instead, she reached out, took his hand and turned to go up the steps.

"Laney."

She stopped but didn't look back at him. Ryker moved up to where she stood, lifted her in his arms and carried her the rest of the way.

"This is more," he told her. "Just let me catch up."

When she laid her head on his shoulder, Ryker knew he was breaking ground on learning how to live with a heart that actually feels. Now if he could only figure out a way to make sure she didn't get hurt...and prove to Braden and Mac that he wasn't just messing around with their baby sister.

Fourteen

Laney was no closer to finding the traitor than she had been three days ago. Her family was counting on her. Their reputation, their…everything hinged on her finding the person who dared go against them. Until they knew who was behind the leak to the Feds, they were each taking turns manning the main office. Laney still wasn't convinced this was where everything went down; the clues the internet was giving her could be deceiving.

Mac and Jenna had decided to stick around through the holidays and definitely until this mess was cleared up.

Working in the office of her ancestors, Laney started looking at keystrokes with a program she'd downloaded. Every laptop in the office had to be checked. They had eight. The Boston office had to be ruled out first. Even though the new offices seemed coincidental in timing, if someone were going to attack, they may do it from close range where they could keep an eye on most of the key players.

Laney reached for another cracker. Normally she'd scold anyone for eating around their computers, but time was of the essence and her little one demanded some food.

"Anything?"

Laney didn't spare Braden a glance as he stepped into the office. "Not yet."

"How are you feeling?"

She hadn't seen him in three days, since the night of the party. He'd texted her to talk work and ask if she was feeling okay, but that was it. Ryker's name wasn't mentioned, and Laney was perfectly fine with that. The more her brothers stayed out of her personal business, the better.

"Hungry. I'm either tired or hungry. It's a cycle."

"Zara is out running errands. I'll have her bring you something."

Laney shook her head. "No need. I practically packed my kitchen in my bag because I knew I'd be here all day and evening."

Braden took a seat across from her. "You can't work yourself to death. You're expecting. I know how tired Zara was."

Her fingertips stilled on the keyboard as she glanced over the screen. "I'm sorry if this hurts you."

Braden shook his head. "You being pregnant isn't what bothers me."

Laney tried to keep the anger at bay. If they were all going to move forward, they had to stay levelheaded and remain calm. And after Ryker had spent the night simply holding her, Laney had a newfound hope that things would work out. They had to.

"You don't want to hear this, but Ryker and I aren't just fooling around."

Braden crossed his ankle over his knee and curled his hands over the sides of the chair. "No, I don't want to hear that my best friend, a guy I call my brother, is taking advantage of my sister. It doesn't sit well with me."

"You think that's what this is? That he's some sex-crazed maniac and I'm his poor, unsuspecting victim?" Laney shook her head and reached for another buttery cracker. "You have no clue, then. I love him."

"Damn it, Laney." Braden jerked forward in his seat, his hard stare holding her. "You're going to get hurt. A guy like Ryker doesn't do relationships. Have you ever wondered why he hasn't had a woman around us? That's not his style."

"It wasn't your style, either, until you got trapped with Zara. Now look at you."

That narrowed gaze didn't intimidate her. She took a bite of her cracker. "If you're done throwing your unwanted opinions around, I have work to do."

Braden came to his feet and blew out a breath. "You're going to get hurt," he repeated, his tone softer now.

"I'm a big girl."

She refused to look at him, refused to give him the power over her, because he had no say in how she handled her emotions or what she did with Ryker.

When he stormed out, Laney let out a breath. *That went well.*

Her cell chimed, but she ignored it. Braden was here, so if there was anything pressing going on, he'd know. The more she looked over this laptop, the more she was convinced it was clean. She'd just shut it down when her cell chimed once again.

Leaning over, she dug into her purse and fished it out of the side pocket. Giddiness burst through her when her contractor's name appeared.

She swiped her finger over the screen to open the message.

Inspections all passed. Moving forward on reworking the electrical.

Finally. Some good news. With the initial building inspections passed, she could push forward and hopefully come in ahead of her original spring opening.

After Ryker had shared his story with her the other night, she was even more determined to raise awareness for children who didn't have a proper home life.

She may not be able to help them all, but if she even helped one, then that was one less child who would doubt his or her self-worth. These kids needed to know someone cared about them, genuinely cared, because that was the struggle with Ryker right now. He didn't know what to do with the love she offered.

Laney sent off a quick reply that she'd be by tomorrow to discuss lighting and a few other questions she had regarding the kitchen area and the rec room.

She was making headway with the project, and possibly with Braden since he didn't seem so full of rage. Now if she could only figure out this puzzle of who was betraying her family. She didn't feel a bit sorry for the person on the other end of this investigation. Whoever had gone against the O'Sheas deserved everything they had coming.

* * *

Ryker had a sinking feeling, and he never ignored his instincts.

As he pulled in front of O'Shea's, he killed the engine and let his mind process all the intel that had come in regarding the scrolls. There were obvious dead ends, so he dismissed those immediately. But there was something eating away at his mind. It only made sense for the works to be fairly close. They were last known to be in Zara's home, or the home that the O'Sheas had lost in the Great Depression. If they had gotten out, word would've traveled.

Braden had searched, Ryker had searched. There wasn't a square inch of that house that had gone uncovered. But Ryker couldn't help but wonder if he'd missed something.

Zara's house sat empty now, well, save for her grandmother's things, because Zara had moved in with Braden. But Ryker wanted to go back in. He refused to give up. He'd been all over the damn globe on hunches, on veiled hints, but nothing had turned up. Frustration and failure were bitter pills to swallow, so he was going back to the point of origin, starting at square one. Because he was fresh out of leads.

Now more than ever, he needed to find those heirlooms. He needed to prove his family loyalties.

He stepped from his SUV, pulling his leather coat tighter to ward off the bitter chill. As soon as he stepped into O'Shea's, Braden's glare greeted him.

"Your eye looks better," he commented before looking back down at a stack of folders on his antique desk.

Ryker didn't take the bait. His eye still hurt like a bitch, but he had no right to complain.

"I want to get back into Zara's house," he said instead.

He moved farther into the spacious lobby area, complete with a Christmas tree that Laney no doubt had a hand in putting up. It had the same damn glittery nonsense she'd wanted him to put in her house.

"That resource is exhausted if you're referring to the scrolls." Braden dropped his pen and eased back in his leather seat. "Why do you need back in?"

Ryker shoved his hands in his pockets. "There's something we're missing."

"You're wasting your time."

"It's my time to waste." He refused to back down on this. "You know I'll just go in regardless. I'm merely telling you for courtesy."

Braden slowly came to his feet. Ryker didn't move, didn't bother to get out of the way when Braden came around the desk and stood toe to toe with him.

"Oh for pity's sake. If this is another pissing contest, count me out."

Ryker caught a glimpse of Laney in the doorway to the back office. Her hair was tied up in a loose knot, and her outfit consisted of an oversize gray sweater, black leggings and brown boots. She looked so young. Granted, she was ten years younger, but the simple outfit had her appearing almost innocent. His heart slammed against his chest as he took in the sight.

He offered her a smile. "I'm just letting your brother know of my plans for the evening."

Rolling her eyes, she moved toward them. "Braden, I think I found something. If you can stop being a bully for two seconds and come look?"

She'd barely gotten the words out before Braden and Ryker were in motion. Once in the office, Laney settled back into the seat, and Braden took one side of her chair while Ryker took the other.

"I found an encrypted email. I had to dig, and the person tried to delete it, but here it is."

"Open it."

Laney shook her head. "I can't. That's the problem. But the subject is damning and it's from the general computer at the main office."

She pointed to the bold header: BACKLOG

"And look at the time and date." She pointed to the screen—it was as soon as the new system was in place. Hours after it had been implemented, in fact. Then they had clearly sent the email and quickly covered their tracks.

The mole was good, but Laney was better. This was the break they'd needed.

"Bastards." Braden slammed his hand on the desk, making Laney jump.

"It's a start," she said, attempting to console him, but there was no calming him. This meant war for whoever did this. "The email wasn't from our internal system, and the account is fake. I just have to dig to find who set it up."

"You can do it." Ryker placed a hand on her shoulder and squeezed. "We all know you can. We're just frustrated and need to get this sorted out before the Feds find something incriminating."

Braden threw up his arms. "They have our sales records. If they search through each and every item, they're going to find questionable pieces."

Feeling a surge of loyalty and protectiveness, Laney glanced up at her brother. "If they searched each piece, they would have speculation at best. I have nothing in the program that indicates where the pieces came from. All of that is stored at my house, in a safe that even you two couldn't crack."

"I'd shoot it." Ryker straightened. "So, you're going to work on this, and I'm going to go back to Zara's tonight. Are you staying with her, Braden?"

Laney leaned back in her seat, looking up at the two men who seemed to be having some sort of staring showdown. She crossed her arms and waited for the testosterone to come down a notch.

"I'm not leaving her alone in her state," Braden replied. "You go. I'll make sure she's fine."

"With all this going on, I think it's safest if she's with one of us at all times."

Braden nodded. "That we can agree on."

Laney jerked to her feet, sending her chair flying back and crashing into the wall. "*She* is right here. And *she* can take care of herself."

They both stared at her as if she'd lost her mind. "I'm serious," she went on. "I don't need a babysitter, and nobody has threatened us with physical harm."

"You're pregnant," Braden growled. "You're automatically vulnerable."

Laney turned to face her brother fully. "You know I'm capable of taking care of myself. Stay all you want, but when I leave, I won't be needing a shadow."

Braden glanced over her shoulder toward Ryker. "Will you tell her? Maybe she'll listen to you."

"She won't listen to me. I ignore her wishes when it comes to things like this anyway."

Yeah, which was how he'd ended up tearing her dress off in a Miami hotel room. He'd been worried for her safety...and then she'd been plastered against the wall, panting his name.

Ryker took her arm, urging her to look at him. Laney shifted her attention. "What?"

"Just listen. For once. I'll be back later. Go to my place. I'll meet you there."

Braden practically growled behind Laney. "Can you two not talk like this?"

"Leave the room," Laney spouted over her shoulder. "I'll go home. If you want to come there, you can. I have too much to do."

Ryker nodded. "I'll try not to be too late."

Once he was gone, Laney glanced back at her over-bearing babysitter. "You know your hovering and child-ish attitude aren't going to make my feelings for him go away."

"I've thought about this. I don't like feeling betrayed, but there's so much more at stake. I want you both to real-ize what's at stake if you fall out. We need him, Laney."

"You think I'm not aware of that? I can't help who I fall in love with, Braden."

He blew out a breath and pulled her into his arms. "Damn it, Laney. I love you both and don't want either of you hurt—even if I'm still pissed at him."

Laney sank into his embrace. "I don't think it's me you have to worry about."

Fifteen

Ryker searched the obvious hiding places at the former O'Shea home once more: closets, cabinets, old trunks. He made his way to the secret tunnel Zara had showed them. The space was rather small and had no shelves, just a chair in the corner. The tunnel could be accessed at one end from an opening at the kitchen and at the other end from the long hallway. Ryker knew if those scrolls were still here, they'd likely be someplace "hidden" like this where no one would think to look.

He ran his hands over the walls. He'd never thought to look for another secret passage. Who knew what surprises this house had concealed? He covered every square inch of the walls, then worked on the baseboards, the floorboards. The tunnel was clean.

He'd been there for five hours and had covered the basement and main floor. There wasn't a loose floorboard to be found. As he went up to the second floor, the steps creaked, groaning against his weight. He froze. Old steps were bound to crackle and settle, but he'd never explored the stairs. Hadn't even crossed his mind—until now.

Ryker went back down the steps and started there. He knocked on the boards, curious if any were loose or sounded different from the others. He tapped each post on the banister, as well. He'd nearly made it to the top when, two steps from the second-floor landing, he hit pay dirt.

He'd been excited before on other hunts only to be deflated when nothing happened. But he was damn well going to devote every bit of energy he had to fulfilling Patrick's dying wish. Ryker owed him at least that—especially because he hadn't been able to stay away from Laney. That was a debt he'd never be able to repay.

Wrapping his fingers around the outside edge of the wood, Ryker gave a slight tug. The wood creaked as it started to give way. The banister that rested in that particular step splintered. Ryker jerked it out, tossed it down the steps…he'd pay to have it repaired later.

His heart accelerated as he gave the board another pull. Finally it ripped free from the step. He eased down another stair and pulled out the minuscule flashlight he'd shoved into his pocket before coming here.

Bending to get a good view, his chest clenched as he spotted something inside. No way could this be the scrolls. The odds that they'd been right under their noses the entire time was pretty nonexistent. Yet something had brought him back to the old house.

Ryker slid the end of the flashlight between his teeth,

then, using both hands, he reached into the space and tugged out a metal box.

Sinking back onto the step, his back against the wall, he stared at the box as if it held every answer he'd ever wanted. Was this them? He wanted to rip into this box to see, but at the same time he wanted to wait, to hold on to the hope he felt right at this moment. If these were the missing scrolls, Ryker had just accomplished what no one else had been able to.

Zara couldn't have known about this hiding spot in the steps or she would've told them. Which made him wonder if her grandmother even knew.

He set the flashlight aside and pulled the lock-pick kit from his jacket pocket. The box was definitely an antique, turn of the twentieth century, if he was guessing right. He'd been working with and acquiring for the O'Sheas long enough to know antiques. This box may be the one the O'Sheas had used before the scrolls had gone missing.

Carefully he went to work on the old, rusted lock. The box was long but not very wide. Ryker wondered if the scrolls could even fit in something this size. Suddenly the lock clicked and the lid flopped open. Most old locks were harder to pick. Clearly this was meant to be.

"Damn," he muttered. There were tubes inside the box. Nine tubes to be exact. Nine tubes that possibly held the nine scrolls.

Ryker couldn't get into one of the tubes fast enough. He'd barely pried the lid off one when his cell went off.

He ignored it. Nothing was more important than this right here. He didn't want to pull anything out, because if these were the scrolls, they'd be beyond delicate. But once the lid sprang free, he grabbed the light again and angled it inside the cylinder.

This was it. He'd found them. Finally.

There were no words, there was nothing but a sense of accomplishment unlike anything he'd ever known. He'd done it. After years, decades of hunting, Ryker had been the one to find the heirlooms so important to the O'Shea family.

Quickly, but with care, he put everything back into the box.

Glancing at his watch, he realized he'd been at Zara's longer than he first thought. It was late, dark, but there was no way he could let this moment pass. He had to let everyone know.

He sent off a quick text to Mac, Braden and Laney, telling them all to meet at Braden's. Mac should already be there, since that's where he was staying, and Laney...well, who knew where she would be. He hoped at Braden's so she could be safe, but knowing her, she went home and was up to her chin in jasmine-scented bubbles.

Ryker had procured many pieces over the years. He'd traveled all over the world. He'd learned languages, used disguises, made enemies all in the name of loyalty and love for this family.

And he was finally coming home with the one true gift he'd always longed to deliver.

"How the hell had we missed this?" Braden asked.

Laney couldn't take her eyes off the tubes. Nine of them lay on Braden's desk. And they were all there to witness this important moment in the O'Shea family history: Mac, Jenna, Braden, Zara, Laney—and Ryker.

She'd never in her life seen him so excited. The pride on his face... Laney couldn't put into words the transformation.

She'd had news to share with them about some antiques at an old estate not far outside the city that they needed to acquire, but that could definitely wait. This moment had been a long time coming. Decades. And here they all were gathered around her father's old desk. Laney couldn't help but feel as if he were here in spirit.

Tears pricked her eyes, but she blinked them away.

"I never even knew that step was loose, let alone came apart," Zara stated. Shock laced her voice as she, too, continued to stare. "I'm sure my grandmother didn't either or she would've told me. She was only a baby when she went to live there."

"Dad was adamant that there were no hidden areas," Braden chimed in. "We knew of the small tunnel that led into the kitchen, but nothing like this."

Braden turned his attention to Ryker and slapped a hand onto his shoulder. "You did it."

Ryker nodded, not saying a word. He may have appeared to have it all together in that typical Ryker fashion, but Laney knew that inside, he was trying hard to keep his emotions in check.

"I had to," Ryker finally murmured, his eyes fixed on the layout. "I owe you all—"

"Nothing," Braden confirmed. "I know I was pissed at you for the whole Shane incident—and I won't even get into Laney—but I see why you took matters into your own hands this time. If you do it again, though, I'll kill you."

Ryker's mouth twitched, but he merely nodded.

"But this is something I honestly never thought would

happen in my lifetime." Braden's voice grew thick with emotions. "Dad would be so damn proud of you."

A tear trickled down Laney's cheek. Zara wrapped her arm around Laney's shoulders, giving silent support. They were all feeling years' worth of frustration, hope, determination, all rolled into this moment. So many leads, so many cities... Ryker had single-handedly trekked all over the globe in an attempt to bring these home where they belonged.

"We need to get these in the safe," Mac chimed in. "Nobody can know they're here, and the security should probably be bumped up."

"I'm already on it." Work mode, that's what Laney could concentrate on. She swiped her damp cheek. "I have an alarm you can put on just the safe. It's sensitive but necessary."

Braden nodded. "Great. How are you doing on the search for our mole?"

"It's got to be one of the employees at the main office." A sick feeling settled in her stomach at the thought of anyone doing this to her family. "That narrows it down to six. Viviana is the newest employee, but I almost feel she's too obvious. Maybe whoever is doing this is using the timing of her coming on board."

Braden carefully capped the narrow tubes and placed them all back into the shallow box. "Keep everyone working on a regular schedule."

"What?" Mac questioned.

"Keep the enemies close," Ryker added. "Now that we know it was one of them, Laney can keep an eye on everything they're doing on our system."

"And they won't have a clue," she added with a smile.

"This is my favorite part of work. Oh, also freezing assets. I do enjoy knowing our enemies are broke."

Jenna laughed. "I'm so glad I'm on your good side."

Laney couldn't help but widen her smile. "You're safe. The DeLucas on the other hand…"

"What did you do?" Braden asked, his hand resting on the now-locked box.

With a shrug and a surge of pride, Laney met the questioning gazes of her brothers and Ryker. "Merely closed some credit cards, possibly drained their off-shore bank account."

Ryker's eyes widened, his nod of approval giving her another burst of excitement. No way was she going to let them get away with the petty little game they played with Ryker. Braden said no more violence, fine. She didn't get involved with that part anyway. But she could sure as hell ruin someone's life. Hard to keep being a jerk when you were broke and powerless.

"I swear, you scare me sometimes," Braden added. He came around Ryker and gave her a brotherly hug. "Just be careful. I know you make sure things can't be traced back to you, but I still worry. Especially now that you're pregnant."

Laney patted his back, meeting Ryker's gaze over Braden's shoulder. "I'm fine. The only time I'd ever been in physical danger was with Shane."

And thanks to Ryker, Shane was a nonissue.

Laney stepped back, smoothing her sweater over her torso. "Since we're talking work, I have a house out in Bradenton that has several antiques that could be of interest. The owner actually called me today asking if we could come look and discuss adding them to the spring show. I'll give you a heads-up. The price they're want-ing is a bit over what I would estimate. But I haven't seen them."

"I'll go." Ryker shoved his hands in his pockets. Laney wondered if that penny was still there after his emotional purging session the other night. "Now that the scrolls have been found, I won't be so tied up and consumed with them. I'll do something normal for a change."

Laney held her breath while Mac and Braden stared at Ryker. After all that had happened—her pregnancy, find-ing the scrolls—Laney prayed her brothers kept Ryker in their brotherhood.

"You do that," Braden finally said. "Good change of pace for you, and it's only thirty minutes away."

Laney let out the breath she'd been holding. "I'll let them know you'll be there the day after tomorrow."

"All this excitement has me exhausted." Zara circled the group until she came to stand next to Braden. The look she gave her husband implied that she was more than ready for their company to leave. "Ryker, thank you, and please don't think a thing about tearing up the staircase."

Shifting in his stance, Ryker rubbed a hand over the back of his neck. "I'll fix it, you have my word."

"I'm going to head on home," Laney told them all. "I'm pretty tired, and it's way past my bedtime."

She gave her brothers a hug, said her farewells to Jenna and Zara, and when she turned to Ryker, there was no mistaking that hard look he gave her.

"Fine. You'll drive me home, and I'll get my car to-morrow. You don't even have to say it."

"Just to make sure she's safe," Mac chimed in.

Laney whirled. "Not now. We've had a good night. Let's not get into another pissing contest. His eye still hasn't healed."

"I can speak for myself," Ryker added. "I'll take her home, and from that point it's nobody's business."

Braden opened his mouth, but Zara elbowed him in the side. "You love them both. Let them figure out their own relationship."

Braden kept his eyes on Ryker, but Ryker only let out a slight grunt. "I get it," he said, holding his hands up. "If I hurt her, you'll bury me, nobody will find me. You all are the only ones who would look anyway."

Laney placed her hand on Ryker's arm. "Braden and Mac will get over it. We're having a baby. Let's focus on that for now."

She couldn't help but borrow his earlier verbiage. Everything that was happening between her and Ryker was going minute by minute. That's the only way her brothers could take it, as well. Besides, how could she tell them what was going on, where she and Ryker were headed, when she didn't know the answers herself?

Silence surrounded them, and Laney was beyond done with all this veiled testosterone tossing.

"Get her home safely," Braden finally said before Laney could open her mouth.

"That's what he's done for years." She had to remind them of how loyal Ryker truly was. And wasn't that ridiculous? He'd been around for decades and had proven himself over and over. "Ryker isn't the one who betrayed you. Remember that."

Laney marched from the room. Still thrilled about the scrolls, she tried not to let her brothers' archaic attitude ruin her mood. She didn't care where Ryker took her, his house or hers. She intended to show him just how thankful she was about his discovery.

Sixteen

Whether it was due to the euphoric state of finding the missing scrolls or the fact that he held Laney until she fell asleep, Ryker didn't know, but he'd been unable to relax in her bed. Last night, after they'd left Braden's house, Ryker had every intention of going to his place, but Laney had nearly crawled in his lap in the car, suggesting they go to her house because it was closer. Who was he to argue?

Now he wished he were anywhere else. As he sat in the middle of one of the spare bedrooms, Ryker glanced at all the pieces to this crib. How did all of these damn pieces go together? The picture on the large box in the corner showed what he should end up with, but he'd never built a crib before. Hell, he'd never built anything. His hands had always been used in other not-so-innocent ways.

Ryker glared at the directions, trying to make sense of the pathetic diagrams. Why the hell didn't the company just send someone to assemble the damn thing when you ordered it?

He'd known she'd been looking at furniture, but until he'd walked past the spare bedroom this morning on his way to get coffee, he'd had no idea she'd actually bought a crib. He couldn't sleep and didn't want to wake Laney, so he figured he'd give it his best shot.

He'd stood in the doorway so long just staring. It had never occurred to him where the nursery would be—her house or his. Both? This was where things started to get even murkier. He didn't want to concentrate on all the reasons this path he was on could go wrong.

Yet he couldn't help himself. The level of comfort he was settling into with Laney was hinting at something so much more. He'd spent nights in her bed, the selfish jerk that he was. Ryker just couldn't tear himself away. He'd mentally pushed Laney away for so long, for so many reasons—his childhood was crap and didn't know how to do a relationship, her father had trusted Ryker to always do the right thing, Laney was ten years younger. The list went on and on, pounding away at Ryker's mind.

Frustrated at his insecurities, he pulled over two of the long boards and a pack of screws. That took no time to put together. Perhaps this wouldn't be such a pain and he could have it done by the time Laney woke up.

The sun hadn't even come up yet, so hopefully she'd sleep a little longer. She needed it. Their baby needed it.

Maybe if this crib got assembled, and didn't fall apart, he'd take her out to pick out something else she wanted. He hadn't gotten her a Christmas present. Hell, what would he even get her? She was all sparkles and grace, and he was a wolf in an Italian suit when his leathers wouldn't suffice.

Their worlds may have collided and run parallel for the past several years, but that didn't mean they were on the same playing field.

By the time Ryker got to the sides of the antique, white sleigh-style crib, he was ready to chuck the entire thing out the window and buy her one already assembled.

"I was going to have someone come in and do that for me."

Ryker jerked around. Laney stood in the doorway, her silk robe knotted around her still-narrow waist, her dark hair tousled all around her shoulders. A lump settled heavily in Ryker's throat. How could he take the mob princess and attempt to fit into her world? Not physically, but mentally. He was a damn mess inside, and he didn't need to pay anyone to tell him that.

"Why aren't you asleep?" he asked before turning back to the mayhem that posed as a baby bed.

He wasn't sure how long he'd been in here, but he needed a break. Ryker came to his feet, brushing his hands on the boxer briefs he'd slept in.

"The bed was lonely," she told him, raking her bedroom eyes over his nearly bare body.

Her smoldering looks never failed to make his body stir. The need for her had never been in question. If all of this was physical, if she wasn't Patrick O'Shea's daughter, hell, if she were anybody else, none of this would be in question.

"What's that look about?" She tipped her head to the side and crossed to him. "You found the scrolls, but you still look as if the weight of the world is on your shoulders."

Maybe because it was. The baby, the need to want Laney in his life more... Ryker wasn't even getting into how Braden and Mac still didn't approve. That he could handle. It was the rest of it he wasn't sure of.

"Ryker?"

He closed his eyes and willed his demons to stand down, but they were rearing their ugly heads even harsher than usual.

"We need to take some time—"

"What? Are you seriously going to tell me you need time?" Laney crossed her arms over her chest. "Don't be clichéd, Ryker. I already told you I was waiting for you, that I'd be here for you."

At least one of them was strong right now.

He ran his hands through his hair, his eyes burning from lack of sleep. "I can't get this damn thing together."

"The crib?" Her brows drew in. "This isn't a big deal."

It was everything.

"Do you know my father threw a glass table at me when I was seven?" he asked, needing her to understand. He ran a fingertip along the scar on his chest. "A piece ricocheted off the wall and hit me here. That wasn't the only time he lost his temper, Laney."

"And you think this is going to change how I look at you? Because you're nothing like him."

With a snort, Ryker shook his head. "I'm exactly like him. You do know what I've done for your family for years, right? When you were learning to write cursive in school, I was already doing all the dirty work."

Her eyes narrowed. In a move he didn't predict, she reached up, planted her palms on his bare chest and gave him a shove.

"If you're going to be a coward and worry about losing

your temper with me or our baby, then get out. I won't wait around for you when you're acting like this. I know the man inside, but clearly you have yet to meet him."

Her rage shattered him. "Are you willing to take the chance? I've never done the traditional family thing, and I have one good memory of the first twelve years of my life. That's all."

"Then you should be more determined to make memories with your child."

Could he? Was that even in him? He had no clue what children wanted. All he knew was what Laney deserved.

If you love it, set it free.

He stared at her, willing his feet to move, to go into her bedroom and get his things so he could leave. But the pink in her cheeks, the hurt in her eyes and the grim line of her mouth were hard to ignore.

"You have to know I'm distancing myself for the sake of you and the baby." He wanted to reach out and touch her. To let her know he did care, too much, but he had to get inside his own head and sort things out. "I need to know you're safe. That's been my role for so many years, but now I need to know you're safe from me."

"Safe from you? Then stop hurting me," she cried, tears filling her eyes. "You can walk out that door anytime, but don't think it's revolving. You know I love you, damn it, you love me, too. I can see it. You wouldn't be so hell-bent on pushing me away otherwise."

Now he did reach for her, taking her hands in his, holding tight when she tried to jerk away. "There's so much inside me that I need to deal with. Everything hit me so hard all at once…"

Damn it. He shook his head, glancing down to their joined hands. "Your father, your brothers have been the only family I've ever loved. But there's still that demon inside me that is the twelve-year-old boy who wasn't given love and security. I need to get that under control before it controls me."

"It's already controlling you." Now when Laney pulled, he let her go. "You have shut yourself off from real feelings for so long you have no idea how to handle them. You found the scrolls, fulfilled your promise to my father, and now you have all this space in your mind that is filling back up with doubts."

She was so dead-on. There was nothing she hadn't hit directly.

Pulling the V of her robe tighter, she glanced away. "Just go, Ryker. You want to. You want to run and hide and be secluded from anything that threatens you to step outside of your comfort zone."

Damn it, she was his comfort zone. He just knew if he stayed in that space too long, he'd end up destroying it if he didn't get a handle on his past.

"For now, this is for the best." He leaned down to kiss her on the head, but she stepped away, her eyes blazing at him.

Swallowing back his emotions, he moved around her and went back to her bedroom to get dressed. He only prayed he was making the right decision because he wanted Laney, wanted their baby. But he couldn't pull them into his world when he couldn't even handle living in it himself.

So maybe going back to Southie wasn't the best of ideas. But Ryker figured if he wanted to rid himself of the past, he'd need to tackle it headfirst.

So here he stood outside his old apartment building.

The place looked even more run-down than he remembered, and he hadn't thought that was possible. The gutter hung off one side, the wooden steps were bowed, the railing half gone. There was no way this could be deemed livable because if this was the outside, he didn't want to know what the inside looked like.

Snow swirled around him. The house next to the apartments wasn't faring much better, but someone had attempted to brighten it up with a strand of multicolored lights draped around the doorway.

Shoving his hands into the pockets of his jeans, Ryker stared back at the door that led to his dilapidated apartment. For the first twelve years of his life, he'd called this place home. He hadn't known anything different. Much like so many of the kids in this area. Granted, some kids had a happy home life because money wasn't the key to happiness. Having a home that was falling apart was definitely not the same as having an addict father who didn't give a damn.

The penny in his pocket brushed the tip of his fingers. Ryker honestly had no clue where his father was now; he didn't much care, either. Most likely the man had killed himself with all the chemicals he put into his system.

Ryker had actually shed tears after Patrick's death, but felt absolutely nothing when he thought of his biological father.

This place did nothing but bring back memories Ryker hated reliving.

He turned, heading down the street. He'd parked a block away, needing the brisk walk. Keeping his head low to ward off the chill, he headed back to his SUV, which stuck out like the proverbial sore thumb. When he was a kid, if this big, black vehicle had come through, Ryker would've thought it was the president himself.

He'd just stepped off the curb and crossed the street when he noticed movement out of the corner of his eye.

"Mr. Barrett?"

Ryker glanced toward the old building that had sat vacant for several years. It used to be a store of sorts, then a restaurant, and he'd just assumed it would be torn down.

"I thought that was you."

Ryker eyed the man who was unlocking the door to the building. After getting closer, Ryker could see it was Mr. Pauley, a popular contractor around the Boston area. The O'Sheas had used him a few times in the past. The truck behind Ryker's vehicle bore the familiar emblem from Mr. Pauley's company.

"How are you doing, Mr. Pauley?" Ryker called.

"Good. Good. Did you come by to check on the property?"

Confused, Ryker stopped by his car. "Excuse me?"

"Miss O'Shea said she'd be by today." He tugged the door open and held it with his foot as he shoved his keys back into his coat pocket. "I figured since you were here, she sent you."

Miss O'Shea? Laney? What the hell was going on?

Ryker was an O'Shea by default, so there was no questioning why the contractor would think such a thing. Everyone around the area knew full well who the infamous family was, and who Ryker associated with and now called family.

Deciding to play along and figure out what Laney was up to—though after this morning he had no right—Ryker headed toward the open door. Once the two were inside, Ryker glanced around. The place was empty, save for the cobwebs that could only have come from tarantulas, some old boxes and some loose flooring.

"As I told Miss O'Shea the other day, I'm reworking the electrical." Mr. Pauley walked through the space and kept talking as if Ryker knew exactly what was going on. "I'm not sure about the kitchen. I may need to rewire some things in there, especially for the appliances she's wanting to use. This building is definitely not up to par for the two ovens she's suggested."

What the hell was Laney going to do with a building in Southie? Ryker continued following the middle-aged man toward what he assumed was the kitchen.

"She's got in mind she needs to crank out several meals a day. I admire her gumption, but this is going to take a lot of money to keep going."

Glancing at the cracked countertops, a rusted refrigerator, a sink that used to be white, Ryker started spinning ideas in his head. And all of them revolved around the perfectly generous Laney.

"But if anyone can help these kids it's her. Patrick was determined to save people." Mr. Pauley glanced back to Ryker with a side grin. "Anyway, this outside wall would be the best location for the ovens, but the wiring is all off. It can be run here. It's just going to cost more than the initial estimate I gave her. Same with the ventilation. Not much more, but—"

"I'll cover it."

His head was spinning, his mind racing over what could have possibly gotten into Laney's big heart that made her want to do this.

Damn the emotions she forced out of him. She wasn't even here and he was facing things he didn't want to. He was feeling so much…and he wasn't as afraid as he used to be. She'd come into his old neighborhood, she was renovating this old building to help kids…just like he used to be.

But he'd told her about his sordid childhood only days ago. There was no way she could've set things in motion that fast—no matter what her last name was.

Something twisted in Ryker's chest, some foreign emotion he almost didn't want to put a name to. The weight of this newfound feeling seemed to awaken something so deep within him, Ryker wondered how long he'd suppressed everything that was bursting through him now.

His entire life.

Ryker tried to focus back on what Mr. Pauley was saying as he pointed and gestured toward various parts of the spacious area that would become Laney's ideal kitchen.

Whatever Laney wanted, he was completely on board.

Seventeen

For the second time in as many weeks, Ryker had made a purchase at All Seasons. Now he stood outside Laney's house feeling like a fool. Perhaps this wasn't the way to go about things. Maybe he'd blown his chance when he flipped out over the crib and let all those doubts ruin what they had going on.

Since he left yesterday morning, she'd only texted him once, and that was to remind him of the home in Bradenton. He hadn't gone yet; there were more pressing matters to attend to.

For the first time in his life since becoming part of the O'Shea family, he was putting work on hold.

Because he didn't feel like he deserved to walk right in using his key, he rang the bell and gripped the shopping sack in his hand.

He didn't wait long before the door swung open. Laney

didn't say anything, and he waited for her to slam the door in his face. To his surprise, and relief, she stepped back and gestured for him to come in.

The warmth of her home instantly surrounded him. She had a fire in the fireplace, her tree sparkled with all the lights he'd put on it. This was home, a perfect home for their child to be raised in.

"Did you get to the estate?" she asked, brushing past him and heading back toward the kitchen.

"This is more important."

Laney stopped in her tracks, just as she hit the hallway off the living room. Her shoulders lifted as she drew in a breath and let out a deep sigh. When she turned, Ryker didn't waste any time moving toward her. He was done running, done hurting her, hurting them.

"I brought something for you." He extended the sack, smiling when her eyes caught the name on the side. "You can open it now."

She quirked a brow, kept her eyes on his and reached for the bag. Laney fisted the handles and stepped aside, sinking into the oversize chair. With the bag in her lap, she pulled out the tissue paper. Ryker shoved his hands in his pockets, waiting for her reaction, hoping he'd gone the right route in winning her back.

When she gasped and pulled out a white-and-gold stocking, her eyes immediately filled. That was a good sign…wasn't it?

"There's more." He nodded toward the bag and rocked back on his heels.

She pulled out another stocking, then another. Tissue paper lay all around her, the stockings on her lap as she stared down. Ryker couldn't see her expression for her hair curtaining her face.

Unable to stand the silence, he squatted in front of her.

"I don't have a fireplace," he started, reaching for one of the stockings. "I was hoping we could hang these here."

When she tipped her head to look at him, one tear slid down her cheek. "You put my name on one and yours on the other."

Ryker lay the smaller stocking over the larger ones. "And this will be for our baby. We can have the name put on once we know it."

"How did you…this…I don't even know what to say."

Speechless and in tears. Ryker was taking all of this as a very good sign. But he also knew Laney wouldn't be so quick to let him fully in. He'd been so back and forth, he needed to lay it all on the line and explain to her just what he wanted. Holding back was no longer an option.

"I hope you don't mind. I made a few adjustments to your plans with Mr. Pauley."

Laney's eyes widened as she sat up straighter. Her mouth formed a perfect O, and she continued to stare.

"I went back to my neighborhood, thinking maybe I could settle those demons once and for all." Before he would've gotten up to pace or avoided looking at her face, but he reached for her hands instead. "Mr. Pauley thought I was there to meet with him since you mentioned going by today."

"I…I called him a little bit ago but got his voicemail."

Ryker squeezed her hands. "Why did you start this project, Laney?"

"I wanted to make a difference for some kids." She glanced down at their hands, a soft smile adorning her mouth. "I started this before you ever told me the full story of your childhood. I'd heard enough over the years and always wanted to do something of my own. When I thought about what you went through, I would get so upset. I thought opening a place for kids to come after school would be ideal. They can get help with home-work, we can feed them. In the summer, they can play basketball, interact with other kids and hopefully stay out of trouble."

She kept talking until Ryker put his finger over her lips. "You humble me, Laney O'Shea. Those kids are going to love this, love you."

Reaching out, he tipped up her chin with his finger and thumb. "Not as much as I love you."

The catch in her breath had Ryker easing forward, closing the space between them as he covered her mouth with his. He stole only a minor taste, promising himself more later.

"I do love you, Laney. Maybe I always have, but I was damn scared of it." She laughed, her eyes sparkling with more unshed tears as he pushed on. "You knew it, and I'm sorry it took me so long to catch up. But I have this past that sometimes threatens to strangle me and I… I'm working on it, but I can't work on my own. I need you, Laney."

She threw her arms around his neck, crushing the stockings and tissue between them. "I don't want you leaning on anyone else. Because I need you, too."

"I want to be here, with you." He eased back but didn't let go. "Your house is warm, it's perfect for our baby, for us. Our family."

"You want to move in here?" she asked, her eyes wid-ening. "My brothers—"

"Aren't welcome. This is about you, me and our baby. Your brothers have an issue, they can take it up with me. I love you, Laney. I've never loved another woman. I want to be a team with you. All of the things I worried exposing you to, you've understood all along."

Laney's hands framed his face as her eyes searched his. "All of this came from you discovering my project?"

"The project just opened my eyes," he told her. "But why didn't you tell me?"

Laney shrugged, nibbling on her lip. "I didn't tell anyone. I told you I wanted something just for me. I'll tell the guys later, but I didn't do this so you all would be proud. I'm doing it for the kids."

Ryker settled his hands on her belly. "You're going to be the best mother. I can't wait to be a family with you."

Laney rested her forehead against his. "We're already a family."

Epilogue

"And who are you again?"

Ryker wasn't about to let just anyone into Braden's home. They were in the middle of a celebration. After a month of tiptoeing around the fact he and Laney were living together, the brothers had finally come to realize that Ryker and Laney were a done deal.

But it wasn't so much their relationship they were celebrating. Zara was pregnant again, and Mac and Jenna were closing in on their wedding date. There was plenty to be happy about...except this visitor at their door.

"I'm an investigator. Jack Carson."

Investigator. More like a nosey jerk with too much time on his hands.

"And what do you want?" Ryker asked, curling his fingers around the edge of the door and blocking the narrow opening with his body. "We have attorneys, so if you have an issue—"

"There's been a fire at the home of Mr. and Mrs. Parker in Bradenton."

Ryker froze. "A fire?" He'd just talked to them two days ago. They were still haggling over prices for their antiques. The young couple with a new baby had inherited the estate and all its contents, and they were hoping to earn some money by selling the larger pieces.

"You seem stunned by the news," Carson stated. "You wouldn't know anything about the fire, would you?"

Shocked, Ryker bristled. "How the hell would I know about it since you just told me? Are they all right?"

The investigator's eyes narrowed. "They were killed. Only the baby survived because the nursery was in the back of the house."

Ryker's gut clenched. The thought of an innocent baby without a mother and father was crippling.

"I hate to hear that," he said honestly. "Why are you here telling me this?"

Braden came up behind Ryker and eased the door wider. "Something wrong?"

Ryker nodded to the unwanted guest. "This is Jack something-or-other. Claims he's a PI."

"What's he want?"

Jack went on to explain the fire while Ryker studied the man. There was something about him that was familiar. Despite the expensive suit, the flashy SUV, the man smelled like a cop. But cops didn't make this kind of money, neither did the Feds. This guy was definitely suspicious...and ballsy for showing up here.

"That's terrible," Braden replied once Jack was done with the story. "I'm not sure where we fit in."

"We're just trying to find who set this fire because it appears to be a cover-up." Jack's assessing eyes kept shifting between Ryker and Braden. "There was a robbery, and most of the antiques were wiped out. The couple actually died from gunshot wounds."

Ryker remained still. "Why don't you quit dancing around the reason you're here and just spit it out."

"The O'Sheas had been talking with this couple, correct? About taking some of these antiques to auction?"

Ryker narrowed his eyes. "Our business is none of your concern."

"It is when there are two dead bodies."

Braden took a step onto the porch. Jack instantly backed up, but merely crossed his arms as if he was bored.

"Get the hell off my property," Braden growled. "If you have a problem, take it up with our attorneys. We don't talk to random strangers accusing us of something we know nothing about."

Braden took a step closer, and Ryker wondered if he'd have to step between these two.

Nah. It was nice seeing Braden get so fired up.

"What cop sent you?" Braden asked.

Jack remained silent and tipped his head. The cocky bastard was seriously getting on Ryker's nerves. Having had enough of this nuisance, Ryker stepped onto the porch and wedged a shoulder between the two.

"While this is fun and all, we actually have lives to get back to," Ryker told Jack. "So you're here of your own accord? No Fed or cop sent you? Then get your nosey ass off the property."

Clenching his fists at his side, Ryker tried to compose himself. But if this guy didn't budge soon, he wasn't going to be responsible for his actions.

Finally, Jack nodded and walked back to his car as if he'd been here for a flippin' Sunday brunch. Arrogance was a hideous trait to witness.

Once the guy was gone, Ryker turned to go back inside, but Braden hadn't budged. He was still staring at the spot where Jack's SUV had been parked.

"Don't let him get to you," Ryker stated. "It's a shame about that couple, but they can't pin any of that on us when we didn't do it."

Braden shook his head. "Did you see his eyes?"

"What?"

Braden looked to Ryker. "That guy. Did you look at his eyes? They seemed so familiar."

Ryker agreed. A shiver crept up his back. He didn't like when he got this feeling. Things never ended well.

"I don't think he was a PI." Braden ran a hand over the back of his neck and started heading toward the house. "We'll talk to Mac later, but for now keep this little visit between us."

Ryker fell into step beside him. "We need to watch our backs. Who knows who the hell this guy is."

It was hard for Ryker to put the mysterious man out of his mind, but when he walked into the house and Laney met him in the hallway, he found himself smiling. She had the slightest baby belly, only visible when she wore something tight. Today she had on a body-hugging dress with tights and boots. She was so damn sexy.

"I wondered where you went," she told him. "Who was at the door?"

Braden moved on into the living room, leaving Ryker and Laney in the foyer. "Nobody important," he replied.

They hadn't discovered the mole, yet, but it was only a

matter of time. Ryker wasn't giving up on bringing down the culprit who was hellbent on destroying the only family he'd ever known.

Laney's arms looped around his neck. "If you're done celebrating here, I'm ready to go home and celebrate privately."

Ryker whispered in her ear exactly what they would be doing in private, and Laney melted against him.

This was his woman, his forever family. They'd been his all along…all he'd had to do was reach out and claim them.

* * * * *

Don't miss the first two
MAFIA MOGULS *from Jules Bennett!*
For this tight-knit mob family,
going legitimate leads to love!

TRAPPED WITH THE TYCOON
FROM FRIEND TO FAKE FIANCÉ

And pick up the sexy and emotional
BARRINGTON *trilogy from Jules Bennett*
Hollywood comes to horse country—
and the Barrington family's secrets are
at the center of it all!

WHEN OPPOSITES ATTRACT
SINGLE MAN MEETS SINGLE MOM
CARRYING THE LOST HEIR'S CHILD

All available now from Harlequin Desire!

If you're on Twitter, tell us what you think
of Harlequin Desire! #harlequindesire

MILLS & BOON®
Hardback – November 2016

ROMANCE

Di Sione's Virgin Mistress	Sharon Kendrick
Snowbound with His Innocent Temptation	Cathy Williams
The Italian's Christmas Child	Lynne Graham
A Diamond for Del Rio's Housekeeper	Susan Stephens
Claiming His Christmas Consequence	Michelle Smart
One Night with Gael	Maya Blake
Married for the Italian's Heir	Rachael Thomas
Unwrapping His Convenient Fiancée	Melanie Milburne
Christmas Baby for the Princess	Barbara Wallace
Greek Tycoon's Mistletoe Proposal	Kandy Shepherd
The Billionaire's Prize	Rebecca Winters
The Earl's Snow-Kissed Proposal	Nina Milne
The Nurse's Christmas Gift	Tina Beckett
The Midwife's Pregnancy Miracle	Kate Hardy
Their First Family Christmas	Alison Roberts
The Nightshift Before Christmas	Annie O'Neil
It Started at Christmas...	Janice Lynn
Unwrapped by the Duke	Amy Ruttan
Hold Me, Cowboy	Maisey Yates
Holiday Baby Scandal	Jules Bennett

MILLS & BOON®
Large Print – November 2016

ROMANCE

Di Sione's Innocent Conquest	Carol Marinelli
A Virgin for Vasquez	Cathy Williams
The Billionaire's Ruthless Affair	Miranda Lee
Master of Her Innocence	Chantelle Shaw
Moretti's Marriage Command	Kate Hewitt
The Flaw in Raffaele's Revenge	Annie West
Bought by Her Italian Boss	Dani Collins
Wedded for His Royal Duty	Susan Meier
His Cinderella Heiress	Marion Lennox
The Bridesmaid's Baby Bump	Kandy Shepherd
Bound by the Unborn Baby	Bella Bucannon

HISTORICAL

The Unexpected Marriage of Gabriel Stone	Louise Allen
The Outcast's Redemption	Sarah Mallory
Claiming the Chaperon's Heart	Anne Herries
Commanded by the French Duke	Meriel Fuller
Unbuttoning the Innocent Miss	Bronwyn Scott

MEDICAL

Tempted by Hollywood's Top Doc	Louisa George
Perfect Rivals...	Amy Ruttan
English Rose in the Outback	Lucy Clark
A Family for Chloe	Lucy Clark
The Doctor's Baby Secret	Scarlet Wilson
Married for the Boss's Baby	Susan Carlisle

1016 GEN STD LP

MILLS & BOON®
Hardback – December 2016

ROMANCE

A Di Sione for the Greek's Pleasure	Kate Hewitt
The Prince's Pregnant Mistress	Maisey Yates
The Greek's Christmas Bride	Lynne Graham
The Guardian's Virgin Ward	Caitlin Crews
A Royal Vow of Convenience	Sharon Kendrick
The Desert King's Secret Heir	Annie West
Married for the Sheikh's Duty	Tara Pammi
Surrendering to the Vengeful Italian	Angela Bissell
Winter Wedding for the Prince	Barbara Wallace
Christmas in the Boss's Castle	Scarlet Wilson
Her Festive Doorstep Baby	Kate Hardy
Holiday with the Mystery Italian	Ellie Darkins
White Christmas for the Single Mum	Susanne Hampton
A Royal Baby for Christmas	Scarlet Wilson
Playboy on Her Christmas List	Carol Marinelli
The Army Doc's Baby Bombshell	Sue MacKay
The Doctor's Sleigh Bell Proposal	Susan Carlisle
The Baby Proposal	Andrea Laurence
Maid Under the Mistletoe	Maureen Child

MILLS & BOON®
Large Print – December 2016

ROMANCE

The Di Sione Secret Baby	Maya Blake
Carides's Forgotten Wife	Maisey Yates
The Playboy's Ruthless Pursuit	Miranda Lee
His Mistress for a Week	Melanie Milburne
Crowned for the Prince's Heir	Sharon Kendrick
In the Sheikh's Service	Susan Stephens
Marrying Her Royal Enemy	Jennifer Hayward
An Unlikely Bride for the Billionaire	Michelle Douglas
Falling for the Secret Millionaire	Kate Hardy
The Forbidden Prince	Alison Roberts
The Best Man's Guarded Heart	Katrina Cudmore

HISTORICAL

Sheikh's Mail-Order Bride	Marguerite Kaye
Miss Marianne's Disgrace	Georgie Lee
Her Enemy at the Altar	Virginia Heath
Enslaved by the Desert Trader	Greta Gilbert
Royalist on the Run	Helen Dickson

MEDICAL

The Prince and the Midwife	Robin Gianna
His Pregnant Sleeping Beauty	Lynne Marshall
One Night, Twin Consequences	Annie O'Neil
Twin Surprise for the Single Doc	Susanne Hampton
The Doctor's Forbidden Fling	Karin Baine
The Army Doc's Secret Wife	Charlotte Hawkes

MILLS & BOON®

Why shop at millsandboon.co.uk?

Each year, thousands of romance readers find their perfect read at millsandboon.co.uk. That's because we're passionate about bringing you the very best romantic fiction. Here are some of the advantages of shopping at www.millsandboon.co.uk:

* **Get new books first**—you'll be able to buy your favourite books one month before they hit the shops

* **Get exclusive discounts**—you'll also be able to buy our specially created monthly collections, with up to 50% off the RRP

* **Find your favourite authors**—latest news, interviews and new releases for all your favourite authors and series on our website, plus ideas for what to try next

* **Join in**—once you've bought your favourite books, don't forget to register with us to rate, review and join in the discussions

Visit **www.millsandboon.co.uk**
for all this and more today!